Big Coulee

-

A Charlie LeBeau Mystery

Gregory L. Heitmann

For my Mom and Dad.

A Charlie LeBeau Mystery

Many thanks to my family, gracias!

As always, a big thank you to my editors:

Angela

Dorene

Gwyneth

Front cover design by: Gregory L. Heitmann
Back cover photo credits: USDA, Google Earth, and the author

Author's Note

This is a work of fiction and the usual rules apply. The characters, the conversations, and the incidents portrayed in this novel have been invented by the author. Nothing in this book is to be construed as real. Any resemblance to actual events, or persons, whether living or dead, is coincidental. Again, none of the characters are real. This is a fictional story conceived for entertainment purposes only.

A Charlie LeBeau Mystery

Other novels by Gregory L. Heitmann:

Fort Sisseton – Dakota Territory

Chief Red Iron – The Lakota Uprising

The G MANN 2 – Pay-2-Play

Teener Baseball

Long Hollow – A Charlie LeBeau Mystery

Buffalo Lake – A Charlie LeBeau Mystery

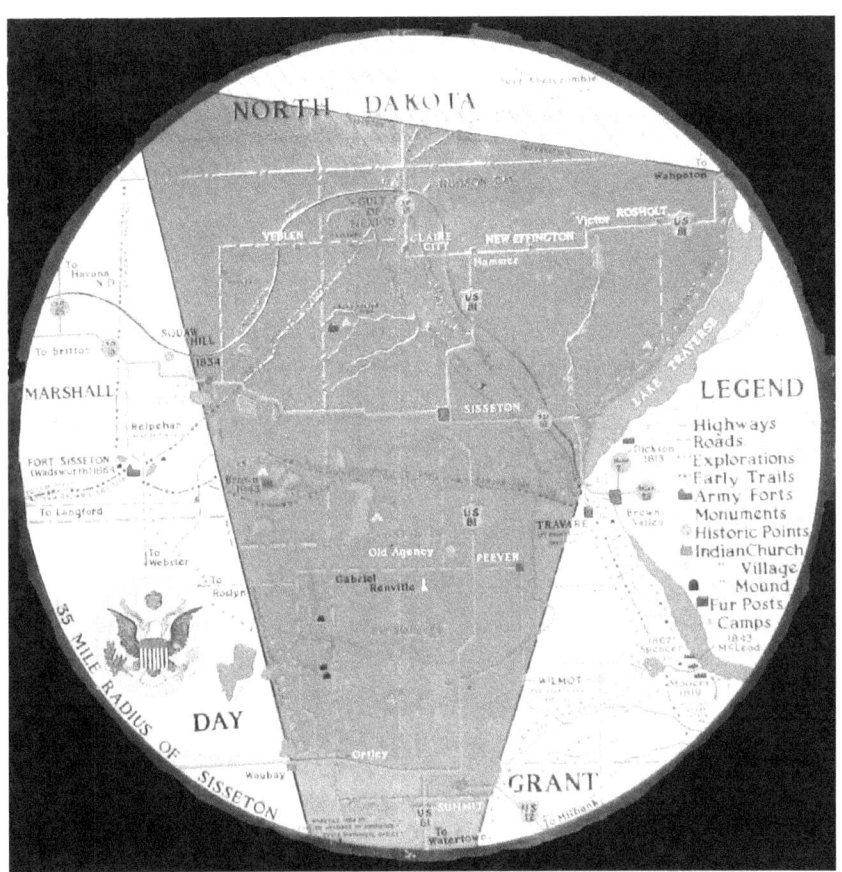

Sisseton Area Map

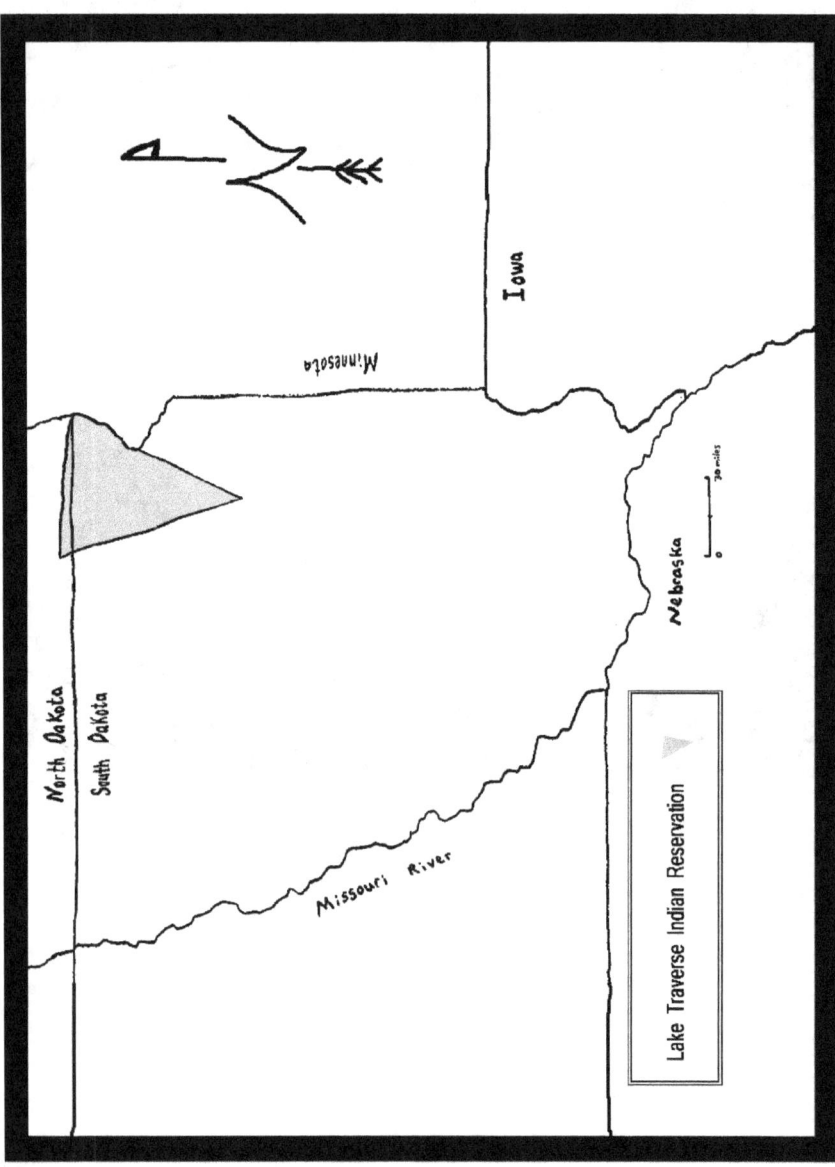

Coulee – (koo'-lee) noun [1800-10 Americanism, <Canadian French, French, Latin> 1. Chiefly Western U.S. and Western Canada. A deep ravine or gulch, usually dry, that has been formed by flowing water.

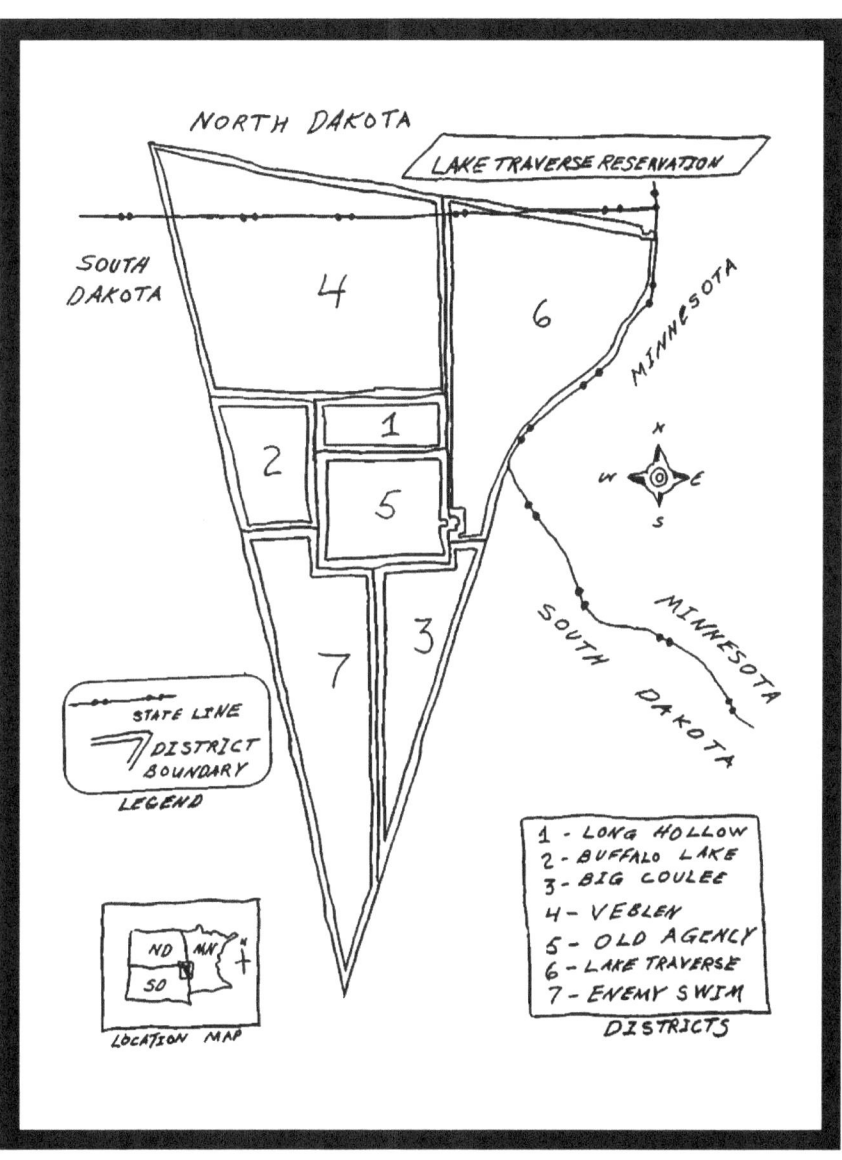

Lake Traverse Indian Reservation Districts

Chapter 1

Teal's Market

Sisseton, South Dakota

The grocery store parking lot is a primary hub of the Lake Traverse Indian Reservation, a.k.a. the Sisseton-Wahpeton Indian Reservation, and Charlie LeBeau heads to his Bureau of Indian Affairs Police Tahoe having just exited the store. Teal's Market generates the most sales tax revenue in Roberts County, and this morning's business bustles. Plastic bag in hand, Charlie is dressed in his BIA police sergeant's uniform as he nods and waves to other customers moving through the parking lot heading for the store entrance. A middle-aged man calls out, "Hey, Charlie."

Charlie can't recall the man's name, but his face is familiar. "Morning," Charlie replies.

As a law enforcement officer in a relatively small community, it seems everyone knows your name. Charlie is used to that fact for the most part, but it still catches him by surprise sometimes. Charlie LeBeau was born and raised here on the Sisseton-Wahpeton Indian Reservation. He is an enrolled member of the tribe, but you wouldn't know it by looking at him. He is the proverbial tall, dark, and handsome man; his appearance dominated by his French-Canadian heritage as his surname would indicate. One might say that Charlie has that familiar, rugged but comfortable look of the middle-aged man in a Cadillac car commercial. The forty-five year old man could pass for thirty, but today he feels his age with a nagging sore throat. He digs through the plastic shopping bag and extracts a sixteen ounce container of Minute Maid orange juice. Arriving at his BIA vehicle, Charlie has the cap of his orange juice off and gulps down half the bottle. The acidic OJ burns his throat. As he lowers the bottle, his eye is drawn to the far end of the parking lot where he spots a toddler. "Hmm," Charlie grunts a reaction to both the sight of the three or four-year old girl and the burning in his throat.

An older Native American woman passes. "Good morning, Charlie."

Again, Charlie recognizes her face, but doesn't know the woman's name. "Good day," he responds with a tip of his baseball cap.

Charlie's attention returns to the far end of the parking lot where the little girl is kneeling, picking dandelions all by herself. Something is definitely not right. He notes the distant looming hills of the Coteau Des Prairies to the west. It is a picturesque sight bathed in the yellow morning light of a low sun. A small girl daintily picking flowers with the morning light on the hills in the background is an image that reminds Charlie of a scene Monet might paint...if he were alive today and living in Sisseton. Charlie absorbs the beautiful view on his mid-morning break as he drinks his orange juice.

The Coteau Des Prairies is a dominant feature on the reservation located in the northeast corner of South Dakota. Glaciers leveled lands to the east and west of the Coteau, literally translated from the French word "slope." The slope of the prairie is a remnant landform from the glaciation ten thousand years ago. The hills didn't suffer the same fate of being ground into rich, tillable soils that contribute to the breadbasket of the country. Instead, the tree-covered slopes and surrounding hills are more suited to ranchers and their pastures. The prairie potholes and lakes are for the outdoorsman. The Coteau Des Prairies is a sportsman's paradise with fishing, hunting, and outdoor activities year-round. The few hundred feet difference in elevation provides a quirk in the climate. The hills are known for more precipitation, more wind, and more extreme everything when it comes to the weather.

Charlie appreciates the view a little longer and quietly thinks to himself how lucky he is to be able to live in God's country. The reservation and hills have shaped his life, and he is content, at least for this moment...except for the tingling pain in his throat. He reaches for his neck and rubs the side of his neck, the spot that burns inside his throat. Charlie drains the rest of the orange juice with a resounding, "Ah," as the burn continues.

He recaps the bottle, tosses it in the bag, and flips the bag onto the passenger seat as he opens the door of his truck and climbs in. "Let's go see what this is about," he grunts the words as he gets behind the wheel.

The grocery store sits perched on a mound of fill brought in to level the area and make the lot suitable for construction. The modified terrain makes it relatively isolated along South Dakota Highway 10. The south side of the building's lot slopes away to an intermittent stream at the bottom of the hill. A few hundred yards to the east of the grocery store, the Coteau Des Prairies Hospital sits atop the adjacent knoll on the opposite side of the drainage.

Firing up the vehicle, the FM radio softly plays Linda Ronstadt's cover of Smokey Robinson's hit "Ooo Baby Baby." Charlie flicks the radio off and mumbles to himself, "Well, that song's a little too on-the-nose."

He drives his vehicle across the oversized parking lot to within twenty five yards of where the girl is kneeling. She is undistracted by the vehicle, focused solely on picking dandelions. Charlie exits the Tahoe and walks to edge of the asphalt parking lot and squats just a few yards from the girl. He can see she is about four years old and very dirty. Her matching, tiny orange sweat suit outfit is grimy, and her face is smudged with what appears to be grease. "Hi, what's your name?" Charlie questions.

The little Native American girl's head snaps toward Charlie in surprise, noticing the kneeling man for the first time. She pauses from her chore of picking dandelions. Charlie notes she is humming some sort of children's tune, *Itsy, Bitsy Spider* he thinks. She sports a boyish bobbed haircut. Her black hair is matted and unkempt. Her dark complexion with rounded, chubby face is true to her Sioux roots. The toddler looks back down and picks another dandelion, "Denise."

"Where's your mommy?" Charlie questions softly.

The little girl points to a clump of thorny brush about halfway down the slope, forty yards from where Charlie kneels. "Let's go see her," Charlie mumbles the words as he stands and extends his hand towards the girl. "My name is Charlie. I'm a policeman. You are safe with me. Do you know what a policeman is?"

Denise nods and extends her hand, grabbing Charlie's. "Policemen get bad guys and take them to jail."

"Yes," Charlie nods as the girl leads the way down the hill. "That's right."

With one hand full of bright, yellow dandelions and the other holding Charlie's hand, Denise does her best to move down the slope. Her steps are that of an uncoordinated child pushing through grass nearly as high as her chest. It's a slow trip down the hill for Charlie as he follows the little girl's lead. He is caught a little off guard as she halts a few yards away from the bushes. Denise stares into the brush, "She's sleeping."

Charlie lets go of his escort's hand and moves forward. He does not see anything in the knee high grass and brush until he is standing over the body of an obviously dead woman. His instincts bring him to a knee as he reaches for the woman's neck and feels for a pulse. She's cold to the touch. The little girl has moved to Charlie's side and is in the process of dropping dandelions one by one on her mother. "Come on, Denise," Charlie whispers as he sweeps the little girl up in his arms as she drops the rest of her flowers. "Are you hungry? Should we get something to eat?"

The little girl nods, momentarily blocking out thoughts of her mother as life's basic necessity of hunger crowds her mind. A last dandelion clinging to her sleeve is tossed away, parachuting down to her mother's body.

Charlie carries the girl as he trudges up the slope in one arm while working with the other hand to free his cell phone from his breast pocket. Halfway up the slope, he presses a button on his phone and holds it to his ear, "Hi, Kathy. It's Charlie. I'm here at Teal's Market. I've got a body just behind the store; can you send assistance?" Charlie listens. "Yeah, wait there's more. I have a little girl here. She's the daughter. She's ok, she's with me now."

Chapter 2

Sisseton

Sisseton, South Dakota, is named for the local Indian Tribe, the Sisseton-Wahpeton band of the Lakota. The reservation boundaries were set by Chief Watoma and agreed upon by the government in the late 1800's. Chief Watoma had stood near where modern day Watertown, South Dakota is, and facing north, he held his arms in a "V" and declared his people's land to be contained in this realm in exchange for peace. The 165-square-mile reservation in the heart of hill country, or "the Coteau Des Prairie," is home to about 10,000 enrolled tribal members. Sisseton is the largest incorporated town on the reservation with just over 2,000 people residing in the city limits with a mix of both Indian and non-Indian, at approximately 50-50.

South Dakota has a strong sense of the four seasons. Typically, the weather is mild in the spring and in the fall, interspersed with hot summers and cold winters. This harsh climate provides a marked cycle of life for the inhabitants of the Indian reservation. The Sisseton-Wahpeton Oyate of the Lake Traverse Reservation is similar to all the Indian reservations in South Dakota. A harsh climate and poverty are two defining traits of South Dakota's Indian reservations.

Part of the trust responsibility of the federal government as defined in the treaties with Tribes is the law enforcement responsibility. The Bureau of Indian Affairs under the Department of Interior manages a police force located on reservations across the country. In Sisseton, South Dakota, the BIA police headquarters and compound is more like a concrete bunker, because it is. It was built in the time of the American Indian Movement (AIM) in the 1970's, and the government constructed a number of ugly monstrosities as defensive positions to thwart future unrest on reservations, but that is a completely different story to pursue at another time.

This beautiful fall day is completely eclipsed for the people inside the BIA police headquarters. The foot-thick concrete walls and limited windows, important to ward off a revolt, make the building dungeon-like for its employees, where presently Captain Skyler "Skip" Kipp and Kathy Chasing Hawk tend to the care of four-year old Denise in Skip's office.

Twenty-five year old Kathy is a motherly figure. An enrolled member of the Sisseton-Wahpeton Tribe, she has the bubbly personality needed to keep the office running smoothly. Kathy is built like a refrigerator with long, straight, jet-black hair cascading to her shoulders. Her appearance is comparable to a caricature artist's rendering of a Native American woman. Her looks are dominated by her round, oversized glasses and a smile permanently plastered to her face, and this noon, turning into afternoon, is no different. She has cleaned up the little girl and shared her lunch.

Skip's office has become the makeshift daycare, and he comes and goes from his office periodically checking in on the two. Skip is an enrolled member of the Sisseton-Wahpeton Tribe. He is a chipmunk-looking, obviously Native American man with round, chubby cheeks and slight overbite. He is a well respected man, in both Indian and non-Indian communities. Everyone acknowledges his dedication to public service. The fifty-three year old police veteran boasts a nearly thirty year career. He could retire, but he loves his job and probably will never willingly leave.

Skip returns to his office to check on Kathy and Denise to find the pair drawing, cutting stars from papers, and stapling miscellaneous shapes to long sheets of paper taped together. Skip can't help but laugh as he observes his assistant and the little girl engrossed in their task. "Any word from social services?" he asks.

"Nothing yet," Kathy responds not looking up from working her scissors around a star she is cutting from the paper.

It is Charlie's return that gets Kathy's full attention as he enters Skip's office. The administrative assistant makes eye contact with Charlie and immediately sets her project aside, scooping up her cell phone that quietly plays music, Sam Cooke's "Chain Gang."

"Come on, Denise. I have some licorice at my desk. I think we need a snack."

Kathy takes Denise by the hand, and they leave Skip's office. Charlie hands a driver's license to Skip. "We recovered her identification from the scene. Do you know her? Cassandra Hopkins?"

Skip heaves a gasping sigh, "I know Cassandra's mom. I'm not that familiar with Cassandra. Cassandra's mom is Beverly LeCompte. She's one of Betty's cousins. I didn't know that Cassandra even had a kid. Let's get her here ASAP."

"I already sent Jeremy to pick her up. She'll be here in a few minutes," Charlie frowns. "She's your wife's cousin?" Charlie's brow furrows with the question.

"Who knows," Skip shakes his head, "second or third cousin. Heck, we're all related on the reservation." Skip looks at the driver's license in his hand, his thumb rubs the photo image. "She was very pretty. Any indication on how she died?"

"Looks like she took a pretty thorough beating," Charlie pauses, "but nothing to her head and face."

Skip clucks his tongue in disgust. "Domestic violence."

"Yeah," Charlie shakes his head. "No shortage of that on the rez." Skip hands the driver's license back to Charlie. "You want me to call Agent Brown?"

Skip's mind works for a moment as he considers all the steps required and paperwork needed to handle a murder scene on the reservation. His head slowly nods, "Go ahead and do that for me. Do it right away. Sooner the FBI knows about this stuff, the less hostile they seem to be to us."

Charlie half-heartedly grins, "Yeah, they're a paranoid lot. Agent Brown's a good guy though."

A disturbance at the back of the building includes shouts echoing down the hallway. The commotion, accompanied with the scuffling of feet on the tile floor, draws the men's attention. Quick footsteps followed by a curvy Native American woman in a designer sweat suit bursting through the doorway into Skip's office startles the men, freezing them in place for a moment. The woman is Beverly LeCompte. The fifty-one year old woman is desperately attempting to be young. Her makeup is stark, and her long artificially black hair is in a pony tail held by a scrunchy matching her rhinestone-studded pink sweats. She is hysterical. "Where is she? Where is my baby?" She yells. Her shouts ranging from disbelief to anger flow as she bounces from Skip to Charlie. "I want answers! What has happened?"

Jeremy Two Crow enters Skip's office, hands in the air, incredulous with the lady's on-going tantrum. Jeremy is the most recent addition to the Sisseton BIA police force. He is twenty-three years old. He is of slight build, but it is the slender build of a former high school wrestling champ.

Officer Two Crow is originally from Pine Ridge, South Dakota, growing up as an enrolled member of the Pine Ridge Sioux Indian Tribe. He runs his hands over his flattop haircut. "I'm sorry, Skip. She just ran away from me when we got in the building."

Skip raises a reassuring hand to his young officer. He turns his full attention to the hysterical woman who is hyperventilating in his office. Raising both hands, he tries to calm her, "Bev. Bev. You're going to have to calm down." Skip steps forward, enveloping the now sobbing lady in his arms. Charlie looks on, admiring the man's ability to tame chaos. "Your granddaughter is here, safe. But...Cassandra, she...she's dead."

Beverly unleashes an ear-splitting shriek that causes Charlie to flinch and put his hands to his ears. Jeremy is driven out of the office, retreating into the hallway and back to his cubicle, away from the manic woman. It takes a few moments for Bev to recover from the news. Skip holds her tightly, rocking her back and forth and making shushing sounds to try to calm the woman. Suddenly she pushes Skip away. With the flip of a switch, Beverly is fully enraged, flashing a temper the likes Charlie has only seen in drug induced criminals that he has tried to arrest from time to time. Beverly's voice is filled with venom, "It's Rodney!" she growls through clenched teeth. Her voice booms out of the office and echoes into the hall. "That deadbeat, drug addled loser! I know he killed her!"

Skip steps forward, again trying to defuse the situation, but an angered Beverly backs away and swipes at Skip's desk, knocking over a stack of files as she screams. "Why didn't you arrest him? You could have prevented this!"

Beverly rushes toward Skip, fists balled up, but he grabs her hands and begins to shush her, trying to bring calm again. Charlie begins to step forward to intervene, but Skip waves him back. "Bev," Skip speaks soothingly, softly, "You are not going to see your granddaughter unless you are able to calm down."

The woman collapses into Skip's arms, and the anger shifts to sorrow as she wails and sobs as her body shakes.

Chapter 3

Rodney

The lockup is located in the bowels of the BIA police headquarters compound. The jail cells line the walls in the basement, where the lack of natural light might be considered a cruel and an unusual punishment. The cells are bathed in the harsh shadows of the suspended fluorescent lights overhead. The gray walls add their own element of dinginess to the environment. Thirty-five year old Rodney Hopkins rests on his bunk, flat on his back, arm over his eyes. He is the lone prisoner in the jail. Eight cells, four on each side, line the walls. The clang of the first barred gate closing behind Charlie doesn't even make Rodney flinch. "Rodney," Charlie calls out as he approaches the cell.

Rodney, dressed in his orange prisoner jumpsuit, stirs on his bunk. By the time Charlie arrives in front of his jail cell, Rodney is on his feet. His wild, shoulder length hair, is matted and dirty, but manages to blend into his heavy beard. He leans against the bars of his cell, arms dangling through the woven steel rods. "How you doing, Rodney?"

"I'm all right," Rodney shrugs. He speaks slowly, deliberately with a hint of a drawl. It's not Rodney's first stint in a jail; in fact, he's kind of used to it. His hands sport crude prison tattoos. He is non-Indian. He's spent the last seven years in the Sisseton area in and out of the local detention centers and jails. He has been habitually unemployed, except for his illicit pot dealings. His difficulty in finding legitimate work is typical for someone who has spent so much time in jail and has that record follow him throughout his life.

"Sit down. I have something to tell you," Charlie orders, pointing to the bunk in the cell.

Rodney eases himself down to his bunk. "I knew it. They don't have a case against me. When am I getting out?"

Charlie shakes his head, "This isn't about your case." Charlie moves to the edge of the cell. "I'm sorry to have to tell you this...Cassandra is dead. Somebody killed her."

Rodney doesn't react. It's as if he hasn't heard the words. He cocks his head, "What?"

"Cassandra," Charlie speaks softly, "she's dead. She was beaten to death."

Rodney's body shakes as he begins to cry as the words sink in. "What about Denise? Is she ok? Where is she?"

Charlie is reassuring with his tone, "She's fine. Denise is with her grandmother, Bev."

Rodney explodes to his feet. "No, no, no, no, no! You can't leave my little girl with that woman. She's Crazy!" Rodney pulls on the bars of his cell as if to try to bend them and escape.

Charlie staggers back at the outburst. "Denise seems fine. I'm sure you're little girl will be fine."

Rodney shakes his head helplessly, tears streaming freely down his cheeks, flowing into his beard. He begins to pace back and forth in his cell. "No, you can't do this. Bev'll hurt her. She can't be trusted." Rodney stops pacing and extends his arm through the bars of the cell, pointing a finger at Charlie. "You know who beat Cass? It's got to be Beverly."

Charlie scoffs, "That's funny; she said the same thing about you."

"Oh, yeah?" Rodney opens his jumpsuit and exposes his torso. "I still have the bruises to show from the last time she attacked me."

Charlie eyes the discoloration, purple fading to yellow-green, on the prisoner's ribs. "How long you been here?"

Rodney shrugs, "A week...ten days? Please, man, I'm beggin' you. Get my little girl away from that crazy woman! Charlie is silent while he thinks. He stares at the distraught man in front of him. "I seen her, man," Rodney continues his voice shaky. "She goes crazy. She's got a temper." His hands paw through his shaggy hair. "I ain't no angel, but she's got a temper." Rodney's gaze bounces around his surroundings before he continues. He tentatively recalls the story, "I admit I was high." Rodney looks left then right as if trying to share a secret. "I smoke a little weed. Sell a few ounces now and then. You know how it is." Charlie nods. "That's how I got beat up, man." Rodney's head shakes. "I was stoned. I showed up at Bev's house with Cass, and Bev flipped out!" Rodney's hands are back running through his hair. "I couldn't even fight back. That crazy bitch is like some sort of freak with crazy-type strength. She whooped me. Cass was there too, she got the same treatment as me."

Charlie's eyes narrow, and he rubs the back of his neck as he tries to comprehend Rodney's claims. Rodney continues to weep; his stringy hair hangs down, and he stares at the floor. Tears roll off his cheeks and hit the floor. He looks up and locks eyes with Charlie, "You got to do something, man. Don't leave my little girl there."

Charlie poses a question, "Where else can she go?"

The query stones Rodney for an instant before he blurts out an answer, "Anywhere but there! You, what about you? Can you take her?"

Charlie dismisses the request, but the raw emotion of their on-going conversation weighs on him. The passion this man is showing appears genuine, and it frightens him. "You got any relatives nearby? Cassandra got any sisters, aunts...anyone that can take Denise?"

Rodney's head wobbles on his neck. His body deflates in defeat, "No, man. I don't know."

Charlie frowns, "I'll have a chat with social services." Charlie knows that it will be useless. The agency, already saddled with an overload of cases, will be more than satisfied to place the child in the grandmother's care.

Rodney grabs the bars of the jail cell. "Come on, man. Just let me out. I'll get her and keep her safe."

Charlie shakes his head, "Can you get bail money?"

"I don't have money," Rodney laments. "Do you think I'd be here talking to you if I could afford bail?" Rodney bites his lip, "You gotta let me out. She's a monster. All I'm in for is selling a little pot. Just lose the paperwork a few days. I'll make arrangements and then you can pick me up again. Come on."

Rodney is in the full throes of crying again. His body trembles as he grips the bars between himself and Charlie, holding on for dear life to just remain standing.

"I'll see what I can do," Charlie offers stoically.

Chapter 4

Plea

Back upstairs in Skip's office, Charlie faces a stare of bewilderment from his boss as the two men sit across from each other, Skip behind his desk, hands folded, and Charlie in the guest chair. It is dead silent for an uncomfortable amount of time before Skip finally speaks, "Seriously, Charlie? Release him?" Skip's voice goes higher as his questions continue. "What, so a drug addled dimwit can try to raise a little girl?" Skip's head shakes. "I can't believe we are even having this conversation."

Charlie raises his hand as he speaks, "You should go talk to him. You want to talk to him?"

Skip laughingly snorts with his scoffing reaction, "And hear him say whatever he can to try to get out of jail?" He leans forward at his desk, inching closer toward Charlie as if his point will be stronger at close range. "Do you know anything about the guy? I know Bev. She is my wife's cousin. They were raised together by their grandma. They were practically sisters growing up. I know her."

Charlie extends a finger and points it towards the floor. "I saw her flash her temper right here in this office just a little while ago. I can definitely see where Rodney might get his concerns from."

Skip eases back in his chair for his rebuttal. "Come on, Charlie. We just informed her that her daughter was dead. She was upset. How do you think she would react?"

"I'm just calling it like I see it," Charlie frowns deeply. "She was more angry than devastated." His eyes widen. "I'll tell you what; it scared me a little. And now, from what I've heard from Rodney..." Charlie shrugs.

Skip stares sharply at the man sitting across from him, as if trying to burn a hole with his glare through Charlie's skull right between his eyes. "Let me tell you something about Rodney," Skip begins speaking slowly, quietly, just above a whisper. "That upstanding citizen and father, has

31

another daughter." Charlie cocks his head as he hears the words. "Oh, yeah," Skip continues. "She's about eight or nine years old, from a previous relationship."

"What?" Charlie questions, trying to wrap his head around this new information.

"Oh, yeah," Skip nods and his voice rises. "The 'father of the year' down in lock up, he's got another daughter. And this other daughter that he cares so much about, well, he just leaves her with others. Friends. His daughter's friends. Whoever." Skip frowns and shrugs as he finally looks away for a moment before returning his glare to Charlie.

Charlie shrinks back in his chair in disbelief. His eyes turn down from his boss's as they focus on the desk in front of them. His voice is barely audible, "He never said anything about another kid." Charlie's hand falls across his chest, and he rubs his abdomen. "He had bruises all over him. He showed me. He claimed that Bev had attacked him." Charlie's brow furrows, and his eyes again lock with Skip.

"Come on, Charlie." Skip shakes his head. "This isn't like you to side with a guy of Rodney's ilk."

Charlie's face scrunches in a puzzled manner. "Why would he say all this and show me the bruises?"

"What are the odds, Charlie?" Skip's voice is low and soothing. "The guy is likely to say anything to get out of jail. One of his junkie friends probably beat him. You gotta take what that guy says with a grain of salt. He's nothin' but a punk drug dealer." Charlie slowly nods as he listens to his friend and boss. "I assure you," Skip continues, "Beverly will take care of her granddaughter just fine."

Charlie continues to nod, "Yeah, I'm sorry, Skip."

"I'll tell you what." Skip points a finger at Charlie. "Why don't you check on the other daughter? Make sure she's ok. I'll find out where she is and let you know."

Charlie stands. "Yeah. Yeah, that's a good idea." He turns for the door.

"One more thing, Charlie." Charlie halts and turns to face Captain Kipp. "Stay away from Rodney. From now on, I'll talk to him."

Charlie nods.

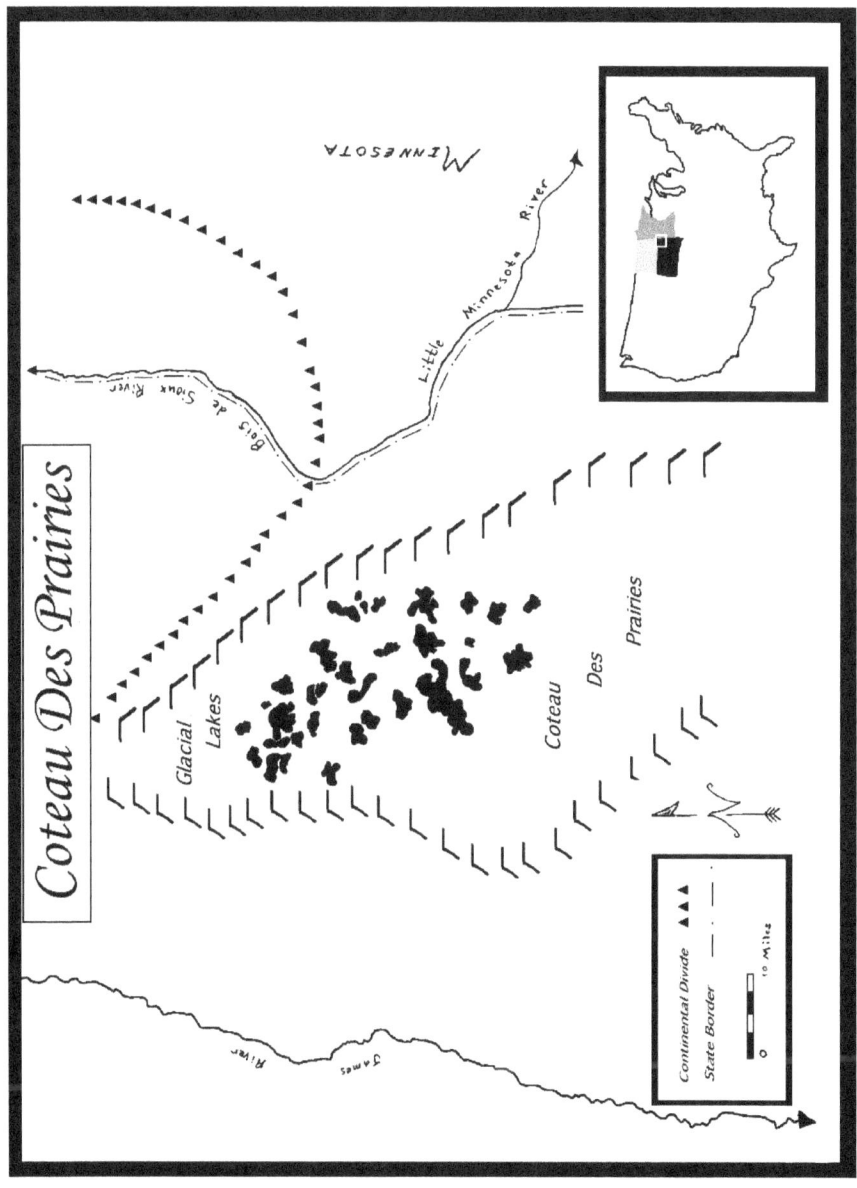

Chapter 5

The Coteau

Charlie enjoys a quiet trip in his BIA police Tahoe as he heads south of Sisseton on BIA Route 7. His FM radio oldies station fills the cab of the vehicle. Buddy Holly's "Well...All Right" fades out and is replaced by Exile and their big hit, "Kiss You All Over." The sun shines down from a cloudless, blue sky, and he takes in the view of the Coteau Des Prairies as Route 7 runs parallel to the hills on his right. Splashes of color dot the hillside as oaks, ash, maples and other trees and shrubs expose their true colors of autumn. Charlie notes that the hills don't seem so imposing in the bright sunshine. The Coteau Des Prairies seems to have many identities depending on the season and weather. Today the slope on the prairie looks meek and unthreatening, even peaceful. Past Agency Village and Tiospa Zina School, Charlie notes a little more traffic and checks the time. School has just let out for the day, cars and buses are on the highway.

Fifteen minutes south of Sisseton, traffic has thinned to nothing, and Charlie turns off BIA Route 7 onto BIA Route 200. He passes an almost generic sign that reads: "Big Coulee District." Near the intersection of Routes 7 and 200, sits the district community building, and Charlie can see a few cars in the parking lot, typical for an after school activity of some sort. Another half mile and Charlie meets a school bus and exchanges a wave with the driver as they pass on the highway. He travels slowly on the highway as he reaches the entrance to the small cluster of government housing units. The street sign indicates Big Coulee Drive. About a dozen homes are built along a street that ends in a cul-de-sac. Charlie pulls around the turn-around and parks in front of a brown cookie-cutter government house. The yard is neatly kept relative to the most of the neighboring homes with patches of grass, but mostly bare dirt and weeds. Charlie looks at the sign next to the front door. It is a chunk of stained and shellacked pine with the name "GERMAN" burned into it. This is the home of Virginia German, an enrolled member of Sisseton-Wahpeton Tribe. Charlie is not here to see her, but her daughter, Courtney. Charlie gathers himself as he prepares to exit the vehicle and talk to a woman he had a brief, but serious, relationship with ten years ago. She is much younger than he is, ten years his junior.

Out of the vehicle and at the front door, Charlie takes a deep breath and knocks. After a moment the door opens revealing a beautiful Native American woman. It is Courtney German, now in her mid-thirties and looking like a model out of a Macy's clothing catalog. Her long, black hair hangs straight past her shoulders and her makeup is impeccable, as if she were a heading to a photo shoot. "Charlie LeBeau?" she questions the man standing before her. Charlie is stunned to silence at the attractive woman before him in the door way. "Hello? Charlie?"

Charlie is finally able to gather himself. "Wow. Long time no see. And I must say, wow."

Courtney smiles, blushing a bit. "What are you doing here? Is something wrong? I'm kinda on my way out the door." She holds the door open. "Come on in. Sorry to be so rude. I gotta get to the casino."

Charlie steps inside, into the compact living room. He stares at Courtney, grinning sheepishly, and she grins back as both note an awkward silence. "How long?" Charlie finally manages. "How long you been back?"

"Been about a year now. Taking care of Mom and working at the casino as night manager," Courtney frowns slightly.

"I thought I saw you there." Charlie nods.

"Yeah, and you never even say 'hello.'" Courtney giggles and taps Charlie playfully on the shoulder. Charlie flushes and Courtney laughs. "I'm just teasing you. It's good to see you."

"So," Charlie continues the small talk, "you're taking care of your mom now."

"Yeah, this is her house, and it's a nice place to live...you know," she sweeps her hand around the room.

"What about...," Charlie begins, but is interrupted.

"Larry?" Courtney questions. "We got divorced. Six years ago already."

"I'm sorry."

"Why would you be sorry," Courtney laughs the words. "You warned me." Silence settles again and the awkwardness causes Charlie to fidget on his feet. "I'm sorry, but I'm going to be late."

"Oh, yeah," Charlie winces, "I'm here...well, this is difficult."

Courtney holds up a hand, "Let me guess. This is about Cassandra and Rodney." She glances to the kitchen, where muffled voices can be heard.

"Yeah," Charlie nods.

"What happened now?" Courtney intones flatly.

"I'm not sure if you heard, but," Charlie heaves a resonating sigh, "Cassandra's dead." Courtney staggers back and Charlie reaches to steady her. "I'm sorry. I thought maybe you heard already."

Courtney looks toward the voices coming from the kitchen again. "Rodney, did he kill her?"

Charlie shakes his head. "He's been in jail; you probably know that. You're probably more familiar with the whole situation than I am. But, it's why I'm here. Here to see Haley." Courtney nods and Charlie continues, "Your daughter is friends with Haley? That's why you've taken her in?"

Courtney nods again. "They're best friends. She's a nice girl. Just in a bad circumstance."

"Social Services is going to come, but is it ok if she continues to stay here for now?"

"I don't see why not."

Charlie nods, "Good. Do you think I can talk to her?"

Courtney nods and sighs. "Brittney! Haley! Can you come here a minute?"

Charlie and Courtney wait in silence for a moment. "How's Nat?" Courtney questions. "I'm sorry about your sister passing."

"Thanks; Nat is good. He is with me. I have my dad with me in my house too."

Courtney grins. "Three generations under one roof. How nice."

Like a whirlwind the ten-year old girls arrive in the living room, breathless at first, without a care in the world. But at the sight of a policeman in uniform, they both recoil, hiding behind Courtney, clinging to each other and Courtney. "Come on, Britt. The policeman needs to speak to Haley."

Brittney is a miniature version of her mother. "But, Mom, we didn't do anything!"

"It's nothing you guys did," Courtney reassures the girls. "It's ok, Haley. We'll leave you alone here in the living room, but we'll be right in the kitchen."

Chapter 6

Haley

Charlie sits side by side on the couch with Haley, on his left, in the compact living room. The room is full with the couch and a recliner that face a small flat screen TV on a stand. The couch is against an interior wall with a view of the street out the room's picture window. The television is off and the room is quiet. Haley stares a thousand yard stare out of the picture window as she absorbs the news. Her voice is flat and hollow as she asks again for the third time, "She's dead?" Her eyes are welling with tears, but she doesn't cry.

Haley Hopkins is a cute ten-year old girl on the verge of the awkwardness of puberty. She is tiny. Her shoulder length brunette hair is distinctly parted down the middle. She is dressed simply, faded blue jeans and a flowery printed t-shirt. She can't seem to comprehend the situation. "You're sayin' my step-mom is dead?"

"I'm sorry," Charlie mumbles, awkwardly patting the little girl's knee. "Brittney's mom says it's ok if you stay here. I know it's not the best situation with your dad in jail. It'll be ok." Charlie pats her hand and squeezes it. "You're sister is ok, too. She is with her grandma."

Haley stiffens and looks to Charlie wide-eyed. It's something that Charlie can't ignore, "What's wrong?" Haley won't answer, turning her eyes down to stare at her shoes. "It's ok. You can tell me. I'm a policeman."

Haley's head turns; her eyes meet Charlie's eyes. Her brow furrows. "Grandma Beverly…she's mean. She hit me…and she hit Cassie."

"You mean she spanked you?" Charlie questions.

Haley frowns and shakes her head. "No, she hit me." She feels the top of her head. "On top of my head. She has a big ring. It hurt."

"Why did she hit you?" Charlie continues with his questions.

Haley's face scrunches. "I don't know. She was mad." Haley frowns and shakes her head. "We were staying with her, and Cassie wanted to paint our fingernails. Grandma Beverly came home and got mad cuz we never asked to use her polish."

Haley is unable to hold back the tears, and they stream from her eyes. She paws at her cheeks, wiping the droplets. "I don't know why she doesn't like me. She doesn't like anyone." Her stare returns to the window. "Why did Cassie have to die? What's going to happen to me?"

Charlie tries to comfort the little girl that seems to be shrinking before his eyes. He wraps her in his arms, and Haley finally succumbs to her emotions. She sobs and Charlie whispers, "It'll be ok."

The crying brings Courtney to the living room. Charlie relinquishes his hug and hands the whimpering girl over to her. Courtney holds Haley tightly and rocks her back and forth. "I'll get going so you can get to work. Sorry." Charlie grimaces as he gestures to Haley. "Sorry to leave you this way."

"It's ok." Courtney nods, her own sympathies cause her eyes to well with tears as she holds the girl still wracked with emotions. "I'll call and tell them I'll be a little late."

Charlie smiles weakly. "If they ask, feel free to tell them it's police business, and they can contact me." Courtney manages to return a half-smile. "Thanks again," Charlie quietly punctuates his response with a nod to Haley. "I'll show myself out," he remarks as he points to the door.

"She'll be fine here with us," Courtney states confidently. Haley pulls herself away. She covers her face and hustles away to the kitchen.

"I'll see you, Haley." Charlie waves at the little girl, but there is no response.

"Girls." Courtney smiles. "She's embarrassed now. She'll be fine. She's a tough kid. A nice kid."

"I think you're right," Charlie says as he half-heartedly agrees.

"It's good to see you. And talk to you, Charlie." Courtney smiles. "You look sharp in your uniform. We should get together. Get a drink."

Charlie flushes with embarrassment, "I'm with somebody."

"I see." Courtney acknowledges the rebuff. "I'm sorry. I'm sorry...I mean. The way everything happened before."

Charlie laughs, "That was a long time ago." A flustered Charlie backs his way to the door. "I gotta go."

Courtney eases to the door as Charlie exits. "Bye, Charlie."

Chapter 7

Pronghorn

Charlie trudges to his vehicle, mumbling to himself. He is embarrassed as he climbs into his police Tahoe, slamming the door. He talks aloud to himself. His voice resonates inside the vehicle. "Geez, Charlie, could you be more pathetic?" He looks into the rearview mirror at his reflection and shakes his head. "A pretty girl gives you a bit of attention and…" He turns the key in the ignition and starts the truck. The stereo plays and Charlie's ear catches the R&B tune "Too Close" by Next. He violently jams his finger on the preprogrammed radio station button. Another song plays. It's "We're In This Love Together" by Al Jarreau. It emanates crisply from the speakers, and once again he jabs at the radio tuner, "…you are the magnet, and I am steel…" soft rock lyrics by Walter Egan fill the air.

"Aurrrgh!" Charlie yells as he turns the radio off. "All you can manage is, 'I'm with someone.' Sad, that's what that is." He puts his vehicle in gear and works to fasten his seatbelt as the truck idles forward to the stop sign at the intersection of BIA Route 200. He looks at his reflection again and shakes his head. "Where is your professional bearing?"

His chastising of himself is over as he waits for traffic to clear, but the vehicle he is waiting for is slowing, window rolled down with an arm out waving for him to follow. It is a Sisseton-Wahpeton Fish and Wildlife truck. Charlie checks traffic and pulls out behind the vehicle and follows it up the Coteau. The Tahoe's engine strains against the steep grade. Charlie is on the tail of the Fish and Wildlife vehicle, puzzled as to why they signaled to him. He observes the fenced pastures dotted with a few cows on each side as they travel up and up. Finally they level off, on top of the Coteau Des Prairie, where Charlie follows the truck onto an approach. The driver is out of his vehicle opening the gate and setting it aside. The man in the straw cowboy hat moves to Charlie's vehicle. It is Bert Taylor, Conservation Officer for the Sisseton-Wahpeton Tribe. Charlie rolls down his window. "What do you know, Bert?"

"Hey, Charlie." Bert frowns as he tips his cap. Bert is a non-Indian. He is a biologist by trade, hired by the Tribe to manage a myriad of hunting and fishing programs. Along with those duties, he is also a law enforcement officer trained in the game and fish regulations, a game warden. "Follow me through this gate and you'll see," Bert's voice strains. He is dressed in his uniform, tan button-up collared, long-sleeved shirt with a badge hooked to his left pocket along with his dark brown denim jeans. He is a contradiction in appearance with a round baby-face emphasized with wire-rim glasses against his ever present straw hat. The "baby-cowboy-warden" is the term Charlie has heard kicked around when referring to Bert.

Bert climbs back in his truck, and Charlie follows him through the gate and slowly, carefully across the rough, chewed down pasture. Charlie spots a couple flicker-tail gophers at their holes ready for escape as the trucks pass. Finally, he can see what looks like white rocks ahead and the vehicles pull up to the objects in the middle of the pasture.

Exiting their trucks, the two men move to one of the objects in the pasture. They stand over and stare down at a dead pronghorn, an antelope. It is surrounded by six other herd-mates, each in various butchered states. Flies crawl and buzz on the carcass at their feet. "What do you think?" Bert questions.

"Poaching?" Charlie asks in disbelief. "When's the last time we had something like this?"

"Not since I've been warden, and that's four years now." Bert turns his attention to Charlie. "Could this be ceremonial?"

Charlie's eyes scan the carnage. The largest pronghorn is missing its head. Three other animals are missing hindquarters and back straps. "I'm not aware of any traditional ceremonies that involve pronghorn or something like this. That was probably a trophy buck." Charlie points at the headless body. Charlie's gaze turns to the east. Below him, from this vantage point the view is spectacular. The flat farmland with different crops, colors and patterns spread out before him. The slopes of hills and the tree-lined drainages meander down the hillside and intersect the flat prairie below where they snake through the cropland forming intricate designs amongst the farm fields. Peever Slough, the wildlife haven for ducks, deer, and their predators rests stoically amongst the crop fields. It's a dichotomy, the slaughtered pronghorn strewn before him and the beautiful scenery of the background.

Bert's head shakes in disgust. "This is ridiculous. We barely have any pronghorn left, and somebody kills half our herd."

"Sad," Charlie comments softly. "I can understand if you're goin' hungry and you need to eat...but, to shoot and leave most of the meat? Some punk kids, I'm guessing."

The warden nods in agreement. "We'll put out a reward. Something will turn up. Almost everyone knows the pronghorn bucks we have around here. Somebody will recognize the horns. Somebody will talk."

"Doesn't give us our antelope back," Charlie's voice is filled with disgust. "We don't even have enough for a hunting season." He scratches his head and looks up into the sky for a moment as he thinks. "I'll bet it's been forty years since they had a hunting season for pronghorn in Roberts or Marshall County."

Bert points to what's left of a pronghorn carcass, just the rib cage on the body, the legs, and head. "You sure it's nothing related to something ceremonial? That one was skinned completely. The only one. Pretty good job."

Charlie clucks his tongue and cocks his head. "I can ask around, but I doubt it. It's not out of the realm of possibility that the one of the pow wow dancers on their circuit killed 'em for an accessory to their buckskin."

Bert snorts a laugh, and Charlie looks at the grinning man. "What?"

"It's funny to me, these questions I'm asking you." Bert smiles and shakes his head. "These are the types of questions I get all the time: 'Do you think it was for a ritual? Did a witch do this? What about a medicine man?'" Bert throws his hands in the air. "I can't tell you all the times when a rabbit is found dead in a yard with its head chewed off by a coyote, I get a call to come out and take a look, and it never fails, somebody wants to know about the spirits." Bert laughs. "Now, look at me. Here I am asking you the same questions."

Charlie laughs, "Hey, this is the reservation."

Bert nods, "We'll get 'em. It'll be poachers. And it will turn out that they are nothing but common criminals."

A Charlie LeBeau Mystery

Chapter 8

Jealousy

Charlie LeBeau Homestead

Just three miles as the crow flies, northwest of Sisseton, Charlie LeBeau's manufactured home sits on a two and one-half acre parcel designated to him by the Tribal Council. His land sits at the base of the Coteau in the Long Hollow District. The tree-lined drainage that runs near Charlie's place flows into Long Hollow when enough precipitation falls. It is a paradise for Charlie. A dream come true to live here. He had had his eye on this acreage since he was about eight years old when he hunted the Long Hollow drainage with his father for deer and turkeys. When he got out of the Army and joined the BIA police force, his first investment was in this double-wide trailer. He ordered it, but it took about a year for his request for his parcel to process through the Sisseton-Wahpeton tribal government's bureaucracy. The petition for his homestead finally made it through, and here he was, just about eighteen years later, a dream fulfilled. To put a cherry on top of his dream, he now was able to share it with someone. For almost three years, Veronica Lewis, the owner, operator, and publisher of the Roberts County Standard had been sharing his life and home...at least part of the time they shared his home. She still kept her house in town for when she was working all hours trying to get the finishing touches on the weekly newspaper.

Veronica is thirty six years old. She is a dark-haired, wholesome beauty from right up the interstate a hundred miles north, Fargo, North Dakota.

Tonight, Charlie smiles as he climbs into bed next to Veronica as she reads with the aid of a nightstand lamp. Veronica looks up from her book a moment before turning her attention back to the page. "What are you smiling about?"

"Nothing," Charlie replies defensively. "I just can't believe you are even here tonight." Charlie settles into bed.

Veronica lowers her book. "What do you mean?"

"I just thought you'd be working on the murder story."

"I guess I needed a break. Besides, I got the new guy to assist me." Veronica closes her book and sets it on the nightstand.

"Chad," Charlie enunciates the name with a sarcastic disdain.

Veronica laughs her words, "What was that tone? Jealous much?"

"Of that guy? Seems like a lunkhead."

"You are jealous," Veronica laughs. "What, just because he played football in college means he's dumb?"

Charlie shrugs, "Hey, he's the one burning the midnight oil, while you're here with me. I thank him for that."

Charlie nestles close to Veronica. She sighs, "It's nice to relax a bit."

Charlie wriggles in closer. "Besides, you're the one who should be jealous. I ran into an old flame today."

"Really?"

Charlie holds up a finger in protest. "Technically, young flame is more appropriate, since she is so young."

Veronica lightly slaps a laughing Charlie on the shoulder. "Gross. How young? You're going to tell me everything. I want to know this part of your history. Enlighten me." She kisses him on the lips.

"Not much to tell. It was ten years ago. She was twenty-ish, and I was thirty-ish. Too big of an age difference. Way too much as far as her parents were concerned."

"She dumped you?" Veronica questions.

"It was a mutual parting...mostly."

Veronica cocks her head. "Tell the truth."

"Well, she left for the University of Minnesota and that was that. I couldn't compete with those young college boys...like Chad." Charlie digs in with a reference to Veronica's new employee, and he receives a light slap on his shoulder.

"Oh, poor thing," Veronica sympathizes sarcastically.

"Her parents were happy. I got over it...several years later when we met." Charlie presses closer.

"How sweet of you to say that." Veronica strokes Charlie's hair, brushing it to one side, and then running her fingers through the tangle of locks. "Where did you run into her?"

"It's part of the murder case. I think I can tell you about it...off the record."

Veronica rolls her eyes at the on-going joke between the journalist and the policeman. "Of course, it's off the record."

"The murder victim's step-daughter is staying with Courtney." Charlie's hands flail above him as he talks, an unconscious habit of his.

"I'm not on this story for the paper, remember?" Veronica whines. "I need you to explain. More details, please."

"Oh, yeah," Charlie laughs nervously now that he is treading into a potentially sensitive subject for both work and personal life. "Rodney Hopkins, husband of the murder victim is in jail. By the way, he couldn't have done it, because he is in jail. Anyway, he also has a daughter from another woman. That ten year old daughter is in his custody. Well, technically not in his custody, because he is in our custody in jail. But, long story short, his older daughter is best friends with Courtney's daughter."

"So, what you're saying is that your old flame's name is Courtney, and she has a daughter."

"Right. You're quite the investigative reporter, but you forgot one thing, *young* flame." Charlie receives another light slap on the shoulder.

"How old is the older daughter?" Veronica inquires.

"Ten."

"What else?" Veronica urges.

"That was pretty much it. I just wanted to check on the older daughter. Her name is Haley. Courtney's daughter's name is Brittney."

"Uhg," Veronica snorts. "What is with all these preppy, White People names?"

Charlie laughs. "I couldn't agree more." He pauses, "So, I was saying I wanted to check on the other daughter. Rodney's youngest by the murder victim. She's four, her name is Denise by the way..."

"I approve of that name," Veronica whispers. "Sorry to interrupt."

"Denise is staying with her grandmother, Beverly LeCompte." Charlie's voice trails off disapprovingly.

"Why did you say her name like that? With such disdain?" Veronica questions with a reporter's curiosity.

"I don't know if I should say anymore." Charlie pushes away from Veronica, but she pulls him back.

"Hey, this is off the record. We are just boyfriend and girlfriend gossiping."

Charlie reluctantly gives in. "All right. I talked to Rodney, the husband in jail, and he had a fit that his daughter is staying with Beverly LeCompte. Her grandma!"

"What? Why?" Veronica flinches. "He doesn't want her with her own grandma?"

"I know it's weird." Charlie's head rocks back and forth on his pillow. "Rodney said that Bev is crazy. Violent even." Charlie sighs uncomfortably as he recalls the conversation. "He begged me not to leave his daughter with her."

"What did you do?" Veronica pries further.

"I talked to Skip."

"And..." Veronica demands.

"Beverly is his wife's cousin. He flat-out defended her."

"What do you think?" Veronica whispers as she strokes his hair.

"Well, that's where we are now. I went to find Rodney's other daughter and that's how I discovered Courtney and her daughter, Brittney...and Haley. Did I tell you that Haley and Brittney are best friends? That's why Haley is staying there."

"Yes, you mentioned that."

"So, I ended up talking to Haley at Courtney's house, and she clenched up when I told her that her step-sister was at Grandma Beverly's. She told me that Grandma Beverly was 'mean' and had 'hit her' before."

"Oh, boy," Veronica whispers the words.

"Oh, boy is right. It's really bothering me."

"Did you talk to Skip again?" Veronica keeps digging.

"I didn't get a chance yet," Charlie's voice fades.

"Do it first thing tomorrow." She clicks off the light, and the room is filled with only the bluish illumination seeping through the blinds from the yard light outside. "I have something to take your mind off all your problems for a bit." She kisses him gently on the lips.

"I got kind of a sore throat," Charlie whispers. "Are you sure you want to kiss me?"

"Just shhh," Veronica hisses as she kisses him some more and Charlie responds.

Chapter 9

Agent Brown

BIA Police Headquarter - Sisseton, South Dakota

Charlie is in a hurry to get to work in the morning, anxious to talk to his boss. His eight o'clock shift starts with an 8:03 A.M. meeting with Skip in the captain's office. "Are you sure?" Skip counters with a questioning, furrowed brow.

Charlie leans forward in his chair opposite of Captain Kipp. "I'm only telling you what I saw and heard. Rodney and Haley both reacted severely when they heard Denise was with her Grandmother Beverly."

"I just can't believe Beverly would be that way," Skip frowns doubtfully.

"This whole situation makes me uncomfortable." Charlie rubs his hands on his thighs nervously. "Can't we just call social services?"

Skip holds his hand up. "Let me go talk to Bev. I'll try to get a feel for what you're hearing. Just don't get things too riled up."

"Thanks, Skip," Charlie sighs, "I'm just worried. I would have trouble sleeping if something happened, and I hadn't said or done something." Charlie stares at his boss and friend. His gaze steels against his counterpart's stare. "I hope you're not offended, her being your wife's cousin and all."

"Never, we got to do our jobs."

The men exchange the slightest of nods, both satisfied with the grave conversation to start their morning. A shadow moves across Skip's doorway, drawing their attention. Charlie emits a laugh, "Hey, look who it is!"

Skip gives a beckoning wave. "Come on in Agent. We've been waiting on you."

Skip and Charlie stand to shake hands with the man dressed in a conservative gray, semi-expensive suit. Federal Bureau of Investigations Special Agent Austin Brown enters the office with a smile. "Took your own sweet time gettin' here," Charlie comments as he releases Brown's hand. "What, the FBI is on a relaxed schedule now?"

The agent is a young version of Tommy Lee Jones, carrying a six-foot frame as one would imagine for a stereotypical government agent. Skip shakes the man's hand, both gripping a little too firmly. "Have a seat," Skip offers, sweeping his hand toward a straight-backed wooden chair.

"Nah," Brown stretches and rotates his torso, trying to loosen his back. "Let me stand a few minutes. That drive from Pierre is getting longer every trip." He leans left then right. "Well, let me hear what you got." Brown rolls his eyes and flips up his hands. "Sheesh, you guys. What is going on out here on the reservation? My boss is chewin' on my butt because of you guys."

Charlie and Skip look at each. Skip nods to Charlie, signaling him to provide the recap. Charlie clears his throat and begins, "Looks like a woman in her early thirties beaten to death...although I'm not positive. I recently had this theory, and, sorry, Skip, I haven't even shared it with the boss."

Skip perks up and turns his attention away from Brown. Brown motions with his hand to continue, "Yeah, go on."

"I had this idea." Charlie rubs his chin. "Maybe she got hit by a car."

"Hmmm," Skip grunts. "You know; you could be right. She never had a mark on her face."

"What I was thinkin' was that she got hit and stumbled her way to the bushes. Maybe on her way to the hospital, but just couldn't make it." Charlie stands up and moves to a map of Sisseton fixed to the wall. The city map is centered between a larger map of the reservation and the famous Animal House movie poster of John Belushi. The black and white poster has been modified. Belushi's character, Bluto, wears a sweatshirt that reads "BIA Police" instead of "College." A photocopied police badge is glued to the left breast of Belushi's image. Finally, a pair of shades and a police hat are drawn on the poster by a black Sharpie marker. The poster is a reminder for everyone that Captain Kipp does have a sense of humor.

Agent Brown's eyes light up as Charlie steps near the poster on the way to map. "I see you've updated the poster. Shades and cap now. Nice."

Charlie and Skip smile briefly, acknowledging the FBI agent's keen powers of observation. Charlie points to the map. "Here's where we found the body. Here's the hospital. Whatever scenario we're talking about, I'm pretty sure she wasn't beaten or injured where the body was found. No signs of struggle. Nothing. She had to have walked there...with her daughter."

"What about the little girl?" Agent Brown pipes in.

Skip shakes his head and looks to Charlie. "She's four," Charlie sighs. "She didn't seem to understand any question we asked. Her mom was sleeping as far as she knew."

Skip looks at the report in front of him and reads a bit, using his finger to guide his reading. "Says here in the preliminary report, 'Victim's injuries indicate death due to internal bleeding.' What we don't know is where the beating occurred," Skip points to Charlie. "Sorry, Charlie. Beating or *injuries*, might have happened."

Charlie taps the map on the wall again. "She could've walked a ways, dead on her feet, in pain, finally succumbing to the injuries and crawling into the bushes."

"Where does she live, where *did* she live?" Brown queries, correcting himself.

"Around," Skip sighs the word. "She didn't have the most stable home life. I think, most recently, she was staying with her mother."

Charlie chimes in directing a question towards Skip, "Didn't Beverly say Cassandra was getting a house in the Tribal housing project out by the Indian Health Service Hospital? I thought she said her house was under construction."

"That sounds right," Skip agrees.

Agent Brown steps toward the map. "What did the mother say about her daughter's whereabouts?"

"Couldn't say," Skip begins to reply. "Or should I say, wouldn't say. Cassie is mixed up in, shall I say, illegal substances."

Charlie points to the floor. "Her husband, who's in our basement lockup, is a small time pot dealer. Cassandra samples the product is what we've heard."

"Husband's been ruled out?" Brown continues with his questions.

Charlie clucks his tongue. "He's been in jail for the past ten days."

"That's a shame." Agent Brown frowns. "The husband is the usual suspect in a domestic abuse case like this. Typically open and shut. What about the husband's compadres?"

Skip shakes his head, "Nothing is turning up. He was small time in his dealings."

Agent Brown scratches his head. "Did you say where the mom lived?"

Charlie points at the map. "It makes sense that she was at her mom's, walking south. Probably headed to the grocery store. Maybe she got jumped." Charlie traces the line on the map from Beverly's house to the grocery store. "If she was coming from her mom's, she would have crossed Highway 10 here." Charlie points to the line on the map representing the highway and taps it. "I still like the idea that she coulda been hit and run over by a car in the dark. She was wearing pretty dark clothes."

Agent Brown shakes his head refuting Charlie's explanation. "What about the girl? She's able to dodge traffic?"

"Maybe her mom pushed her out of the way," Charlie rebuts.

"Even at four years old, I'm sure the little girl would have been able to tell us if something like that happened." Agent Brown's lips pucker as he thinks. "The girl didn't see how her mother was injured. It had to have happened a while before she walked towards the store." Agent Brown looks back and forth between Charlie and Skip. "Do you think I could talk to the girl?"

Skip nods. "Yeah, you can come with me. I'm heading over there when we're done here."

Charlie points to Skip. "Did we mention that Skip is related to the deceased?"

Skip nods. "Cassandra's mom, Beverly, is my wife's cousin."

With a shrug of his shoulders, Agent Brown replies, "Isn't everyone on the rez pretty much related?"

Skip and Charlie chuckle. Skip responds as he pushes away from his desk and stands, "You're not too far off."

"Come on then," Agent Brown moves towards the door. "You can also show me where you found the body."

Chapter 10

One-On-One

The Charlie LeBeau Homestead

Charlie arrives home at the end of the day and parks his BIA police Tahoe clear of the drive way as his nephew shoots baskets on the homemade court. "You ready, Uncle?" Nat questions as Charlie moves up the stairs onto the deck. He pauses by the front door of the modular home. Charlie's nephew, Nathaniel "Nat" Chasing Wolf is already worked up into a sweat as he stands, ball under his arm, grinning at his uncle. Nat is dressed in his typical uniform of white t-shirt and long shorts, so he's ready to play basketball anytime. His facial features are soft and delicate. With his dark complexion on a wiry six-foot-three frame, he has an exotic look. He's well into his second year since his mother passed, a victim of cancer. Nat's father, a policeman, was best friends with Charlie. He died, a victim of a drunk driver, before Nat was even born. Charlie is not only the father figure in Nat's life, he is the competition on the driveway court.

"Let me change," Charlie calls out as he holds on to the door handle and looks at the young man on the driveway below him. He notices Nat's shoulders seem to be getting wider and wider. The much darker-skinned boy has become a fine looking man, just like his father. Nat's father and Charlie had been in the BIA police academy together almost twenty years ago. David Chasing Wolf had shortened his name to just David Wolf. He had been the product of a hard life on the Pine Ridge Indian Reservation and had escaped poverty to become a public servant. Charlie had introduced David to his sister. They had married quickly and soon after, produced Nat. The fairytale romance quickly ended with David's death on duty, victim of an all too common problem of drunk driving on the reservation.

"You ok, Uncle?" Nat calls out to Charlie, who is standing with his hand on the door, thinking about the boy in front of him that has become a man.

Charlie snaps back from his deep thoughts. "Just trying to figure out if I should beat you with my inside game, outside game, or both." He pulls open the storm door, and pushes the main door inside. "I'll be right out."

Inside the house, Charlie inhales deeply, "Mmmm. Smells good. What's for supper, Dad?"

Claude LeBeau, Charlie's father replies with a smile, "Venison roast. Be ready in thirty to forty minutes." Claude LeBeau is seventy-five years old. He is an age-progressed image of Charlie. A shock of white hair, a lined face, and a slight stoop are virtually the only difference between father and son. Claude has played a larger role in Nat's life than most grandfathers. Between him and Charlie, they were Nat's surrogate fathers, shaping the young man in the ways of male culture.

"Forty minutes, good, I'm starved. But, first I gotta school Nat out on the court."

Claude laughs at Charlie's misguided confidence. "Good luck with that. That kid is a machine. He made fifty free throws in a row as I rebounded for him before I came inside to finish supper." Claude moves to the window and watches Nat dribbling the ball between his legs in a figure eight. "Don't hurt yourself, Charlie."

Charlie smiles and shakes his head as he disappears into his bedroom.

*   *   *

The one-on-one basketball game rages on the driveway in a close battle. Charlie is in his shorts and ragged black t-shirt. He sports a worn out pair of Nike Air Jordans. The shoes have seen better days, soles worn to nothing on the rough concrete, which makes up most of the court. A little bit of gravel beyond the top of the key and a little bit of hard-packed dirt on the side of the court round out the playing surface. The front of the house faces west. This time of day the big cottonwood tree with its own soggy depression outside the reach of the coulee, provides much needed shade from the setting sun; however, the thinning leaves of fall aren't doing the job they used to. The sun causes flickering shadows through the leaves and onto the backboard making it even more of a challenge. Charlie holds the ball a moment at the top of the key to catch his breath. He's worked up into a froth now. "How was cross country practice?"

"Good," Nat responds and takes a swipe at the ball in Charlie's hands.

"You run with 'em?"

"Some," Nat takes another swipe at the ball as Charlie pulls it back. "A couple miles. I can't do their five to seven miles." Charlie nods, straightens, takes a deep breath, and bends his knees, exposing the ball for another swipe by Nat. "We do some 300 yard sprints. Six of 'em. That was enough for me."

"Time out," Charlie calls as he rubs his eye and tosses the ball to Nat. "Got something in my eye. There I got it." Nat squares up on defense, waiting before handing the ball over to his uncle. "What else?" Charlie questions, hands out ready to get the ball from his Nephew.

"Tomorrow, they're taking us into the hills. Run up the hollow road a quarter mile and then walk back down. They said ten reps."

"Uf-dah," Charlie grimaces as Nat checks the ball to him. Charlie makes a quick move, passing by Nat, dribbling and spinning as he attempts a reverse layup. Nat slaps Charlie's arm on the shot.

"Sorry. Foul." Nat shakes his head as he clucks his tongue.

Charlie gets the ball back at the top of the key and hands it to Nat to check. "What else do you do as cross country team manager?"

Nat bends his knees and holds the ball. "Mostly make sure the water bottles are filled and help with stretching. Also, got to make sure the shoes got all the spikes. Just basic stuff."

"Good. Nothing like a little work to keep you humble, plus you stay in shape with the running."

Nat starts to hand the ball back to Charlie to continue the game, but their attention is diverted to an ear-piercing squawk from inside the house. They both look towards the house. "Grandpa and his turkey call?" Nat questions.

Charlie snickers, "I hope so. If it isn't, I'm not sure what kind of dying animal we might have behind the skirting and under the house. Is that supposed to be a crow call?"

Nat grins, "Hard to believe it's already time for fall turkey season. Should be easy; they're practically outside the door every morning just milling around."

"You wait," Charlie says as he points to the woods. "They get a sixth sense when the season rolls around."

The front door opens, and Claude emerges with his scratch turkey call. Moving the stylus across the surface of the call, Claude coaxes a yelp that echoes off the side of the house. "Supper time!" he yells.

Charlie stands at the top of the worn key hand-painted on the concrete slab. He turns his attention to Nat holding the ball under one arm, standing at the free throw line. "What do you think? Next basket wins?" Charlie questions.

Nat laughingly scoffs, "Yeah, that seems fair...I'm only up like...six baskets."

"Come on," Charlie cocks his head and pleads sympathetically.

Nat rolls his eyes. "Fine. Check." Nat bounces the ball to his uncle and moves closer, left hand in Charlie's face.

Charlie holds the ball out in front of him, bends his knees, and head fakes to the right. With one bounce to the left, he leaps, launching a picturesque jump shot. Nat is slow to react. Swish, the net snaps like a whip, the ball passing through the nylon, ending the game. The basketball caroms off a corner of the concrete slab and skitters away toward the tree-lined drainage. "Good game," Charlie declares, holding out his hand.

Nat rolls his eyes and smirks as he gives his uncle a congratulatory high five. "Nice shot," he affirms.

"Go get the ball and let's eat!" Charlie points to the ball where it has settled twenty-five yards away. "Hustle," he says with a grin.

Chapter 11

Talking Turkey

The men eat supper at the dining room table. It is all business with only the sounds of silverware scraping the plates for a couple minutes. Claude breaks the silence, his appetite sufficiently at bay. "You guys ready for turkey season? Did you hear my call?"

Nat nods, pausing mid-fork to his mouth. "Yeah, Grandpa, sounds good."

Charlie chimes in, head cocked to the side as he waits to respond after chewing and swallowing. "I hope I can get time off."

"Hmmph," Claude grunts, wiping his mouth with a napkin. "Shouldn't take more than the first mornin'. I think I counted seven Toms right out in our coulee the other morning."

Charlie shovels more venison roast in his mouth, chews, and swallows. He nods his head. "Good roast, Dad."

"Thanks, it was the first doe from last year. Nat got her."

Nat smiles proudly. "I only shoot the good ones. Tender."

"Anyway," Charlie interjects, "I don't know about time off for me. Police work never ends. We got that Hopkins girl now."

Claude heaves a sigh and cocks his head. "So I hear. Sad. I don't know how you can deal with it."

"It's not easy," Charlie comments. He picks at his slice of roast and takes another bite of his crescent roll. "In fact, let's change the subject." He looks to Nat. "How are your classes? Senior year. Sisseton High School. Just like me and Grandpa." Charlie looks to his dad. "Three generations of Sisseton High graduates…if he makes it." Charlie quickly points to Nat and snickers. Nat's only response is a shrug as he keeps eating. "That's it?" Charlie laughs the words. "A shrug of your shoulders? How about using some of those words they're supposed to teach you in English class?"

"Good." Nat shrugs and puckers his lips as he thinks about school so far, his eyes look toward the ceiling a moment before meeting his uncle's. "Yup, good."

"Bravo," Charlie's mocking tone is finished with a laugh. "Remind me to tell the school board that the teachers are doing a fantastic job."

Claude and Nat laugh. "Oh, and by the way, they don't call it English class any more. It's called Language Arts."

Charlie and Claude look at each other with quizzical expressions. "Language Arts? I don't get it." Charlie questions.

Claude finishes chewing, swallows, and holds up his fork. "Political correctness."

"Oh," Charlie responds with an eye roll.

The men eat in silence for a couple minutes. "Pass me another roll, please," Nat requests. Claude obliges, flipping a crescent roll in the air and Nat snags it. "I do have some news," Nat continues. "You guys remember Katherine, on the cross country team? I think I introduced you guys to her at Sisseton's meet the other day."

Charlie and Claude nod as they eat. "What about her?" Charlie inquires.

"Well," Nat begins, setting his fork down a moment and drinking from his glass of water. His cadence quickens as he speaks. "She's talking me up to this girl on Webster's cross country team. Her name is Ann. Anyway, she wants me to go to their homecoming dance. Can I go?"

Charlie frowns. "Webster? I don't know. Claude?"

Claude shrugs. "Kid's gotta learn sometime."

"Learn what?" Nat looks back and forth between his table companions. "Learn what?" he repeats.

Charlie glances to his father a moment before meeting Nat's eyes. "Ever notice that Webster's not too keen on our people?"

"Our people?" Nat flinches.

"Indians," Claude says flatly between bites of his roll.

"What?" Nat's face puckers, not understanding.

Charlie shifts in his seat. "They don't want us there. Webster is ten miles from Waubay and there's not one Native in the school." Charlie's head shakes. "Never had any Indians...heck, when I was in school or since."

"That includes when I was in school," Claude grimaces.

"Hmm," Nat rubs his chin. "I guess I never thought about it."

Charlie and Nat look at each other and there is silence at the table a few moments before Charlie offers softly, "Well, think about it now that you know what we know. I don't believe it's a coincidence. Just think about it before you decide to invest any time in Webster."

Chapter 12

Make a Case

BIA Police Headquarters – Sisseton, South Dakota

Skip, Charlie, Agent Brown, and Jeremy reconvene for a morning meeting to discuss the ongoing murder case. "So, what'd you find out?" Charlie questions.

Skip points to himself, "Me?"

Charlie smiles, "Yeah, I'm looking at you."

Skip redirects his finger pointing toward Agent Brown. "I'll let him tell you."

Agent Brown clears his throat and looks at each man scattered about Skip's office. "That Beverly seems like a real piece of work." Brown directs his attention to Skip. "No offense Skip, you being related and all."

Skip holds up his hand and shakes his head. "None taken. Related only by marriage."

Agent Brown continues, "It was like pulling teeth to get her to let me talk to the little girl alone. Very protective."

"And?" Charlie questions with anticipation.

"Nada," Brown shakes his head with a frown.

Charlie turns to Skip. "Skip, you ask Beverly about Rodney's and Haley's accusations?"

"Sheesh!" Skip deflates, sinking into his chair. "Talk about an ordeal. You would've thought I punched her in the face." Skip shakes his head as he recalls the conversation. "I talked to her while Agent Brown was interviewing Denise. Boy, oh boy, the waterworks. 'How could you think such a thing?' She kept repeating over and over."

Agent Brown examines his peers in the room and heaves a sigh. "Basically, we got nothing."

Jeremy holds up a finger as he stands and walks toward the map of Sisseton on the wall. "Not necessarily." He taps on the map. "I found out that Brooks Motors has security cameras. Right here." He touches the map at the location of the car dealership. "Primitive system, but I got some information." Jeremy traces the likely path of Cassandra, starting at her mother's house to Brooks Motors. "It's not a very sophisticated security camera. Grainy, but the streetlight was good enough to provide illumination. With the timestamp on the tape, I was able to determine she passed by the dealership at about 11:45 P.M. the night she died. She was on foot, little girl in tow."

Agent Brown straightens; he swells with pride gesturing with both hands towards Jeremy. "Hey, now that's what I'm talking about. Good work, Officer. You ever think about the FBI?"

"No, Sir," Jeremy replies without skipping a beat.

"Well, you should," Brown's head dips as he nods to Jeremy. "A fine young Native gentleman like yourself could go a long way in our organization. Diversity, that's our middle name."

"I thought it was 'Bureau,'" Charlie deadpans.

Stifled laughter ripples through the room. Agent Brown glares at Charlie, but he cant' keep a straight face as he cracks a smile. "There's always a smartass in every group."

Charlie grins. "Anyhoo," he breathes the word as he points to the map, "it follows our theory. Either hit by a car, or she was in all likelihood, injured earlier. She didn't know how bad..."

"The video seemed to indicate she was stumbling a bit as she walked." Jeremy pauses. "However, signs point to the fact that she might have been stoned. A partially smoked joint was found in her pocket, and another rolled joint behind her ear."

Charlie is up from his chair, and he moves to the map. "She's injured, fatally, she doesn't know how bad she's hurt. She dies a couple hundred yards from help." Charlie taps the location of the hospital on the map. "Dead in a tangle of bushes just down the hill from the store." He touches the map, indicating where the body was recovered.

"I find it hard to believe," Skip's voice is thick with disgust, "that we can't find somebody that knows her whereabouts that evening. Right now, we still don't know if it was a murder. Coulda just been an accident. A hit and run."

Agent Brown leans against the wall, bouncing his hands behind his back near his waist, pushing off and returning to the wall, as he thinks. "Gotta treat it like a homicide. Just have to keep lookin'."

Jeremy clears his throat. "I got a list of her friends, and I'll be tracking them down and questioning them."

"Again," Agent Brown pulls his hands from behind his back and gestures toward Jeremy. "Look at this guy. We got real police here."

Charlie and Skip shake their heads at the comment. Skip straightens the papers on his desk and stands. "Sorry to run you guys out, but I have to get Betty to the clinic for some blood work."

"Everything ok?" Charlie inquires with concern.

"Just routine tests," Skip smiles. "Knock on wood," he raps the desk top. "Cancer free for six months now."

Everyone mutters congratulations to the captain, and he smiles.

"Good enough," Charlie nods. "Jeremy, you'll be out and about then?"

"Yup." Jeremy holds a piece of paper with a list of names. "I'll be checking off these names of Cassandra's friends. "I'll give you a holler if I find out anything."

Everyone is moving toward the door to exit Skip's office, but Charlie hangs back. "Agent Brown, you got a minute?" Brown nods and pauses, letting Jeremy exit. "Skip, mind if we use your office a few minutes?"

Skip waves a hand toward the desk. "Be my guests. I'm outta here. I'll be back this afternoon."

The room clears, save for Brown and Charlie. Charlie closes the door, and Agent Brown sits in the guest chair opposite Skip's desk. Charlie sits in Skip's chair. "What's up? " Agent Brown crosses his legs and smiles at Charlie.

Charlie doesn't smile back. "It's coming up on two years."

Agent Brown's smile fades into a frown. "Deer Slayer. I know."

Charlie holds up his palms. "Anything? You promised you'd keep me up to speed."

Brown leans back in his chair, deflated. His head moves back and forth slowly. His frown deepens. "Sorry, Charlie. There's nothing. We had that one little blip, but it's like the guy fell off the face of the earth."

Charlie's brow furrows. "I gotta do something. Veronica still has nightmares. PTSD."

Agent Brown nods. "She get some counseling?"

"She's still going twice a month to Watertown."

"Good." Agent Brown gathers himself and leans forward. "And you?"

"Me? I'm fine." Charlie grabs at the center of his buttoned uniform shirt. "She...I...we need closure on this. I think she's never going to completely turn the corner until this guy is behind bars."

Agent Brown twists his mouth before nodding. "Let me rattle some cages up the chain of command and see if anything shakes loose."

"I'd very much appreciate it," Charlie smiles weakly.

A large grin creases Brown's face. "You two still together? Charlie and Veronica?"

Charlie flinches. "Yeah. Why do say it like that?"

"No reason," Brown shrugs. "It just seems like it might be tough...reporter and cop. Conversation always a little stifled."

"We seemed to have worked it out. Believe me, 'off the record' is a mainstay in my vocabulary."

Brown lets loose with a hearty laugh. "Wedding plans?" the Agent's eyebrows bounce inquiringly.

Charlie waves a hand toward the man, brushing away the words. "Nobody's rushing into anything. She's a good reporter. I think she still has designs on advancing. I'm holding her back...really."

Agent Brown leans forward and points a finger at Charlie. "Here's some free advice. You better tie her down. Start a family. That'll quench any desire for taking off. Focus on the family. It's what my wife does." Brown snorts a laugh. "You think my wife has any love for the teeming metropolis of Pierre, South Dakota?" He relaxes in his chair. "There you go. Focus on a family. The best advice you'll ever get. Just look at me. I'm living proof."

Agent Brown nods, satisfied with himself. He leans back in his chair tipping it on its back legs. In an instant, he is too far back, he loses his balance and tips over backwards, crashing to the floor. The ever-stoic agent rights himself and the chair, sitting quickly as if to hold down the unruly chair. He is unhurt, other than his pride. He stands, inspects the chair, and sits again still looking to the chair as if the furniture is somehow defective. Charlie is beside himself as he holds back hysterical laughter for the most part, but unable to completely restrain his mirth, letting a few giggles slip.

"You ok?" Charlie finally questions.

"That was embarrassing," Agent Brown states matter-of-factly. His face is flushed, and he again stands to inspect the chair, and finding nothing, quickly sits. Charlie is awestruck that the man barely misses a beat in the conversation after such a catastrophically awkward event. Brown looks at Charlie. "Where was I? Oh, yeah. She's a city girl, my wife. Pierre, South Dakota, is a far cry from Columbus, Ohio, where we met, but she doesn't even consider it. She spends every waking moment thinking about the kids."

"You might be right," Charlie nods.

"I know I'm right!" Agent Brown raises his voice passionately. "Having a family is great. You think I could put up with all the shitty things we have to deal with if I didn't have my family supporting me?"

Charlie pushes back. "It's a little different for me and Veronica. I got Nat and Claude."

"Nat's gonna be gone in a few months. Off to college," Brown rebuts. "Claude, on the other hand, you got your hands full there."

Charlie laughs, "You got that right."

"Family's the way to go. Don't be scared; jump in with both feet." Agent Brown stands.

Charlie looks up at the man. "I'll think about it."

Brown steps closer to Charlie and slaps a hand down on his shoulder. "One other thing. You aren't gettin' any younger. You know what I mean?" Brown shuffles a couple steps to the door, and Charlie stands, stepping away from Skip's desk and following the agent. Brown turns. "Let me make a couple phone calls. Right now. Maybe light afire on that cold case. I'll let you know what I find out."

Charlie smiles. "Thanks, I appreciate it." He eases to the doorway where Agent Brown stands. The Agent has his back to Charlie looking down the hallway but not exiting.

Brown turns to Charlie. "One last thing."

Charlie steps back, "What?"

"I've heard whispers, couple different places now. Last night at the hotel, the clerk, she mentioned something."

Charlie's eyes narrow, puzzled by the agent's mysteriousness. "What?"

"Well," Agent Brown smiles sheepishly, "there's talk of the ceremonial killing of antelope up in the hills. I was wondering if this is somehow related to our girl's murder. Is there any *dark magic* out there in the Tribe?" Brown shrugs. "I'm just curious." Charlie's look of disdain is enough to answer the question for the agent. "Fine. That's not an angle to pursue."

Charlie shakes his head. "Why does everyone want to reach for some mystical answer to these situations?" Charlie's hands go to his hips impatiently. "There's always a reality, but nobody wants to go there. The simplest answer is usually the correct answer."

"It's just not as dramatic though," Agent Brown whines with a smile. "It's sort of like Bigfoot or UFOs. We can't prove they don't exist and wouldn't it be cool if they did?"

Charlie steps forward and puts a hand on Agent Brown's shoulder, turns him, and eases him out the door into the hallway. "It would be cool. But I not only live on the Indian reservation, I live in reality."

Chapter 13

Britton

Britton Country Club – Britton, South Dakota

Just off the western edge of the Coteau Des Prairie, where the hills have leveled off into an ever so slightly rolling terrain, you'll find Britton, South Dakota. West of Sisseton, Britton is connected by South Dakota Highway 10 as the road winds through and over the Coteau. Britton, although not within the reservation boundaries, is influenced by the Native American culture. Its high school is honored to be known as the Britton Braves. Today, just outside of Britton, a couple miles north and east of town on the golf course, the Braves are hosting a high school cross country meet for their neighboring Sisseton Redmen and other northeastern South Dakota high school teams. Golf games are put on hold for the day, as about one hundred runners, half boys and half girls, will compete on the links, distance running, not chasing a little white ball with a club.

The Britton Country Club is a fantastically designed golf course, given its compact forty-acre limitation. Tight, tree-lined fairways challenge anyone who tees it up. The fairways are lush. The cool weather grasses thrive now that summer has passed, and the rough is a reasonable challenge. There are limited water hazards, but the rolling terrain is competitive, and bunkers will help test your golf skills. However, today, the course is closed, giving way to invading teenagers ready to run.

The wind blows fiercely from the south, a warm fall wind. Not the perfect conditions for golf or running on this blustery day, but as most of the students and coaches would tell you, "It's better than sitting in class!"

Nat is dressed in black sweats, just as the rest of the Sisseton Redmen team wears while warming up and stretching at the team camp. The Sisseton camp is a blanket piled with backpacks and assorted warm-ups that flap in the breeze, periodically breaking away, forcing someone to chase the garment across the fairway. Pete Franklin, a senior for the Redmen, is sprawled on the team's blanket. On his back he stares at the sky as he waits for the girls' race to commence before he gets serious about his warm-up routine. Pete is pale. He is so white he is almost albino. His thin blonde hair waves in the wind. His eyes and mouth stand out from his nearly transparent skin. "Hey, Chasing Wolf," Pete calls out.

Nat is a few yards away. He is standing, providing his friend Katherine something to lean against as she stretches in preparation for her race. She pulls on her toe, maneuvering her foot to her behind, stretching her quadriceps muscle. Nat turns to face Pete. "You say something, Pete? With this wind, I can't hear."

Katherine and Nat move closer to the camp to talk to Pete. Katherine continues different stretches, using Nat to lean against. Pete looks to Nat a moment before staring up at the sky again, watching thin clouds chase through the blue sky. "Your dad say anything about some ritual killing of antelope up on the Coteau?"

"My dad?" Nat flinches.

"I think he means your uncle," Katherine pipes in. Katherine Taylor is a seventeen year old senior. She has the willowy frame of a cross country athlete. Her long brown hair is braided tightly, not succumbing to the gusting wind. Her blue eyes and pinched face make for what could be a young Reese Witherspoon.

Pete props himself up on an elbow and looks at Nat. "Charlie LeBeau, the cop. That's not your dad?"

Nat's eyes narrow as he looks at the boy on the ground. "Charlie's my uncle. My dad died."

"Oh, sorry, man." Pete's eyebrows rise. "I didn't know." He looks away from Nat momentarily, and his eyes widen. "I guess that would also explain why his name is LeBeau and your name is Chasing Wolf."

Nat shrugs it off. "That's ok, and no, my uncle didn't say anything about antelope being killed. What are you talking about?"

"You haven't heard?" Pete flinches and looks around as if he is imparting some sort of secret. "Rumor around town is that the Hopkins woman that was killed and the slaughter of the antelope up in the hills were both part of some Indian ceremony."

Nat shrugs, "Beats me. I haven't heard any rumors. I can ask my uncle."

Katherine back hands Nat on the shoulder to get his attention. "Hey, there she is."

Nat turns his attention to a girl jogging by the Sisseton camp. Pete's and Nat's gaze follow the stunning girl. She is dressed in the maroon and gold colors of Webster High School. She notices Nat and her serious, game-face cracks momentarily as she smiles and gives a wave as her eyes meet Nat's. Nat is mesmerized in the moment; his hand raises unconsciously, providing the slightest wave back to the prettiest girl he's ever seen.

Katherine swats Nat's arm again to get his attention. "Earth to Nat." Nat stares at the girl jogging away not looking toward Katherine. "Does she want to talk to me, or is she already over the idea of someone like me?"

"I'm sure she wants to talk to you," Katherine rebukes Nat's tone. "She wouldn't have contacted me if she didn't. She needs someone to go to the homecoming dance with, and that someone is you. She needs to know soon."

"Woo!" Pete emits a howl. "That girl is smokin' hot! Hey, Nat, if you don't go, put in a good word for me."

Katherine snorts a laugh, and Pete is wounded.

"I don't know; that might be more appropriate," Nat replies looking to Katherine. "I'll talk to her after the race, buy my uncle wasn't too encouraging about me going. He implied Webster isn't too keen on people like me."

"People like you?" Katherine questions, her voice rising in surprise.

"Indians," Nat replies flatly.

"Webster doesn't like Indians?" Katherine questions again, her voice going even higher. "I've never heard that before."

Nat shakes his head as he frowns, casting a glance at Katherine. "Neither had I, but my uncle is not in the business of making stuff up. I'm going to tell her I can't go because of basketball. I don't want it to be a big deal."

Katherine leans more heavily on Nat as she pulls on her other leg. "Oh, that's too bad. Hey, what about Sisseton's homecoming? You interested?"

"Maybe, who's asking?" Nat smiles.

"Hey." Katherine swats him playfully. "I'm asking,"

"You're asking me?" Nat flinches.

Pete jumps at the chance when Nat balks. "I'll go with you." Katherine's eyes roll as she shoots a paralyzing glance at Pete. He shrugs, "Just thought I'd volunteer."

Nat recovers. He is still a little perplexed at the invite. "You're asking me? What about Danny?"

Katherine stammers as bit, "Danny's just a friend. Not that kind of friend...a friend, friend."

"I understand," Nat laughs at her discomfort. "He's a friend. He is gay, right?"

Katherine plasters the most serious look on her face she can manage. "He's not out. And don't either one of you say anything." Katherine gives a death stare to Pete. "He's got to come out on his own terms."

Nat laughs again, "Yeah, it's kind of the worst kept secret in the school."

"Be nice," Katherine orders.

"Yes," Nat finally replies. "Yes, I'll be nice...I always am, and yes, I'll go to the dance with you. It should be fun."

"Yay," Katherine raises her arms in playful celebration.

Nat points a finger at her. "I'll only go with you...that is, if you make sure Danny doesn't have a hissy fit."

Katherine's celebration continues as she playfully slaps Nat's shoulder before gripping his arm in a partial hug. Nat swings his arm around Katherine and pats her on the back. A whistle interrupts the moment. The officials are calling the runners to the start. It is a forgettable race in the blustery winds. Katherine and her friend, Ann from Webster, squeak into the top twenty finishers, respectable positions for their skill level. Some days they compete for breaking into the top ten, but today they run at about their average capability. Nat joins Katherine and other team members on a cool-down jog. As they circle back to the Redmen Team camp, they encounter Ann Van Wyck on her own cool-down jog. With a slap on the back and a push Katherine leaves Nat. "I'll let you talk to Ann."

Katherine jogs away and Nat jogs to Ann's side, and they begin to walk together. "Hi," Ann greets Nat.

"Hi, to you," Nat replies. Ann is even prettier up close, even in full froth after running 2.3 miles. Her jet black hair is closely braided to her scalp to keep it out of her face as she competes. Nat notes that it looks like her hair is ready for a red carpet appearance. Her piecing blue eyes are like nothing he has ever seen before. She is definitely beautiful.

Ann extends her hand. "Ann Van Wyck," she introduces herself formally. Nat grabs her hand. Her voice is even beautiful, like music to his ears.

"Nat Chasing Wolf," Nat replies, smiling and completing the introduction.

"It's good to see you and meet you." Ann's smile turns to a frown, "Unfortunately, I have some bad news. I can't go to the homecoming dance like I told Katherine." She sighs deeply, "I have a college visit my parents want me to take, and their schedules overrule me." Her frown deepens as she explains, "University of Minnesota."

Nat is relieved that he won't have to lie. "Oh, that's no problem."

Before another word can be spoken, a tall, thin, middle-aged man approaches the couple. The man is about the same size as Nat and the two lock eyes for a moment. "There you are honey," the man says as he narrows his eyes in scorn while holding his gaze upon Nat a moment longer before turning his full attention to his daughter. He puts his arm around her. "Good race today. That wind was tough out there."

"Thanks, Daddy," Ann coos. "Daddy, I want to introduce you to Nat Chasing Wolf. He's from Sisseton." She gestures to Nat. "You remember him from basketball? I think he scored thirty five against us last year."

The forty-five year old man's demeanor mollifies slightly. "Oh, yeah. You look familiar." He extends his hand. "Doctor Kelly Van Wyck."

Nat shakes his hand, "Nice to meet you, Dr. Van Wyck."

Doctor Van Wyck pulls on his daughter steering her away from Nat. "Come on, Ann. We got to get back to Webster. I'm on call, and your mom needs your help." He gives a wave to Nat. Ann looks over her shoulder as she is led away by her father. She holds her hand to her head as if it is holding a phone and mouths the words, exaggerating her effort. "I'll call you."

Nat raises a hand in a wave and smiles. He knows this is a futile endeavor and is satisfied; that is that.

Chapter 14

Road Trip

BIA Police Facility Lockup; Sisseton, South Dakota

The new day finds Charlie in the basement. The main gate clangs behind him as he walks down the center aisle of the eight cells, four on each side. Only one is occupied. Rodney is still the only prisoner. He is on his bunk when he finally pays attention to the footsteps that halt in front of his confined space. He springs to his feet as he glances up and realizes Charlie LeBeau is standing outside his cell. "Hey, Boss," Rodney calls out, his voice strong and optimistic. "They goin' to let me out? Let me get my daughter?"

Charlie can't hold back a smile. "Sounds like the judge will have a decision by the end of the week."

Rodney relaxes against the cell's bars. "Oh, thank God. Is she ok?"

"Listen." Charlie leans closer. "I'm not supposed to be talking to you, so I was never here. Understand?"

Rodney nods. "Is she all right though?"

Charlie nods slowly. "As far as I know, she's doing just fine. I'll see later."

Charlie turns on his heels and is marching away. He can hear Rodney's voice ring out behind him. "Thanks, Boss!"

*   *   *

Upstairs, Charlie nonchalantly appears in his boss' doorway. He is feeling a little guilty for having defied Skip's order to stay away from Rodney, but those feelings are kept to himself. "Can you do me a favor?" Charlie asks politely after knocking on the door and entering.

Skip doesn't bother looking up from the report he is reading. "What is it?"

Charlie sits in the guest chair across from Skip. Skip looks over the top of his glasses at a grinning Charlie. "Uh-oh," Skip groans. "When I see that look, I know something is up." The slightest hint of a smile appears at the corners of Skip's mouth.

"What?" Charlie laughs the word. "Seriously, I need you to call your Uncle Titus and see if he's around. I need to talk to him."

Skip's face twists in a puzzled look. "First of all, where would my Uncle Titus be? He's pushing ninety years old, and second of all, why do you need to talk to him?"

Charlie puts on a serious face for a moment, but can't hold it. "Police business," he replies unable to defeat his grin.

"I'm not going to call him unless you tell me what this is about," Skip threatens.

Charlie sighs. "I want to put an end to all these rumors about this murder being tied to those pronghorn slaughtered up on the Coteau."

"Yeah, I've heard that stuff. Ceremonial or sacrificial something or other." Skip nods, biting his lip.

"Yeah." Charlie rubs his chin. "That's what I need to talk to Uncle Titus about. Pick his brain on the old ceremonies. He's one of the last old school guys. A historian. He'll be able to shed some light on any possible connection...I think."

With a barely perceptible nod, Skip springs into action. He picks up the phone and dials the number from memory. He is used to calling his Uncle for routine checks on the old man's health. Uncle Titus Korman is Skip's mother's oldest brother. He lives alone in the small town of Veblen up in the northern part of the reservation. He's lived there as far back as Skip can remember.

The phone conversation is short and sweet. Skip arranges for Charlie to meet Titus at his house in Veblen after lunch. Titus has promised coffee. Charlie smiles and stands, satisfied. "Sounds good, Boss. I'm going to haul my dad along. I was thinking the older generations might spitball some ideas and questions I might not think of, plus my dad needs to get out of the house."

"All right then." Skip sends Charlie off with a nod. "Good luck."

Chapter 15

Seeking Water

It didn't take much for Charlie to convince his dad to go for a drive to Veblen. Visiting Titus would fill the afternoon. After lunch Charlie and Claude make their way mostly north and a little west of Sisseton in Charlie's BIA police Tahoe. It's a quiet half-hour ride with most conversation based on the fields and harvest. Behind the discussion, the FM radio plays, first "The Hustle" by Van McCoy and then another instrumental selection, a smooth jazz tune, "Always There" by Avenue Blue, featuring Jeff Golub on lead guitar. They talk about the fall turkey hunt, but both men agree, they are eagerly anticipating hearing what Titus might say about the pronghorn.

On the south side of Veblen, a small, shrinking farm community at the base of the Coteau Des Prairie, there sits a government housing area for the Veblen District of the Sisseton-Wahpeton Tribe. It is distinct in the fact that the cookie-cutter homes mirror each other on the grid of streets. While the rest of the community has tree-lined avenues, the reservation housing is wide open, save for a scraggly Russian olive tree here and there between the houses. The houses are nearing the end of their life-cycle. Now, they are forty-plus years old and show the wear and tear. A couple houses are boarded up. Multiple lots are vacant, their houses victims of fires over the years. There are no lawns to speak of. Where grass would be, bare ground or the drying stems of kochia weeds rule.

Charlie pulls up in the driveway of Titus' home. "Looks like the Dodge is still here." Charlie points to the 1980's Volare car on blocks set in the front lawn like a decorative statue. Weeds, now fading in the fall season, crowd the rusted vehicle.

"I wonder how much he could get for scrap metal on that old car." Claude questions.

"He'll never get rid of it." Charlie smiles. "It's a landmark in Veblen, especially in the neighborhood. Everybody gives directions according to that car. You know, 'three houses north of the old rusted Dodge.'"

"You're right," Claude agrees.

The blinds move inside the house as Charlie and Claude exit the vehicle. The front door opens in anticipation of their arrival. Titus "Uncle Titus" Korman stands in the doorway, "Come on in, boys; I got the coffee ready!"

Charlie and Claude move up the two concrete steps and into the house. Charlie, the last one in, shuts the door behind him and the house is dark. "Let me open the blinds a bit," Titus calls out in the dark. "I like to keep the heat out, so the blinds are shut during the day." The old man turns the rod on the blind, maneuvering the slats open and letting sunlight into the room. Uncle Titus is shriveled and shrunken. He is stooped but glides around the house spryly for a man pushing ninety years old. "What a surprise to get the LeBeau Clan for a visit. Come, sit. I got coffee."

A black and white cat trails after Titus in the kitchen, nearly tripping the old man as he retrieves a pot of coffee. Charlie and Claude sit at a tiny kitchen table in the compact dining room. The house in total is probably one thousand square feet with the kitchen and dining area accounting for about a fifth of that square footage. Titus pushes the cat away with his foot. "Chompers, scat!" he calls out. The cat circles, confused a moment, then trots to the couch in the living room. It jumps up on the sofa and takes a position watching the men in the dining area, lying on its belly with its paws tucked under its chest.

"I like your cat," Claude notes. "Nice black and white." He turns to Charlie, "Maybe you should get a cat for the house Charlie."

"No, Dad," Charlie replies without hesitation. "Thanks for having us, and thanks for the coffee," he continues as Titus pours coffee in the cups on the table.

"You're welcome, son." Titus takes the pot back to the coffee maker and returns to the table. "So, what's all this hub-bub about pronghorn, thathókala?" Titus pronounces the word pronghorn in Lakota, and it is indecipherable to Charlie and Claude. "Pronghorn, that is how the Lakota refer to the animal."

"Oh," Charlie nods and sips his coffee. "The reason we're here is to ask you about any ceremonies involving pronghorn. Are there any secret traditions?"

"If they were secret, I sure couldn't tell you, could I?" Titus laughs.

"Shadow Dancers. That's what we want to know about," Claude pipes in between sips of coffee. "See, this woman was killed..."

"Dad," Charlie interrupts his father holding up his hand.

"No, it's ok, Charlie." Titus snickers a bit. "It's always looming in the background, the mystical side of death. The mythical Shadow Dancers," Titus rolls his eyes. "People want answers to greater questions than man can ever know." Titus pauses to take a drink of coffee. "From what I understand, that woman was beaten. Man's work. Not spirits or ceremony or tradition. An evil man."

Charlie and Claude listen to the old man talk. It is quiet after he finishes, and Charlie is again confident in his previous conclusions in the case despite others questioning the murder.

"What can you tell me about the pronghorn, anything?" Charlie breaks the silence with his question.

Titus frowns and rubs his face in thought as he searches for words. He shakes his head ever-so-slightly. "There's not much to tell about the old ways. I will show you." Titus pushes his chair back and shuffles to the living room. He scans a large book shelf on the wall next to the modest TV. Extracting a large bound book from the shelf, he returns to the table. Charlie and Claude move their coffee cups, and he sets, what turns out to be a photo album, before them. Flipping a third of the way through the album, he stops at a black and white photo of six Indian men kneeling. Each man straddles a large pronghorn buck. The photo is imperfect, out of focus, but the stoic men are obviously proud. Titus taps the page. "This is the thathókala wóečhuŋ...pronghorn ceremony. It was the Big Coulee's pow wow. Their clan's feast day every year. It's been kind of lost."

"Do you know who these men are?" Claude asks the question, drawing an *I'm-the-policeman-here look* from his son. "Sorry," Claude laughs.

Titus points to the two Indian men at the left side of the picture. Their hair is in long braids, and they look to be in the prime of their adult lives, no more than thirty years old. The grainy photo shows just a hint of yellow but is in superior condition for its age. "These two right here, these were the blood-line of the Seeking Water clan. If I remember right, their names were Ephraim and Mitchell Seeking Water. They were brothers. They're both long dead now."

Charlie whistles. "Wow that is interesting," he shakes his head in disbelief. "How do you even know that, not to mention even remember such a thing?"

Titus grins. "Just one of those things some people get. Sort of a photographic memory, you might say."

"So the pronghorn ceremony," Claude interjects, "it just faded away?"

"As far as I know." Titus looks to the men. "Times have changed, you guys know. At least publicly, there's not a trace left of it." Titus' eyebrows go up. "You might want to ask the Seeking Water clan members. They are still around, but they are scattered. Lake City. Buffalo Lake. Big Coulee. Talk to them; maybe they have their own family traditional ceremonies."

"Huh." Charlie's head nods unconsciously. Ideas bounce in his head as he ponders the dead pronghorn. Maybe the answers will be easier to find than he first thought.

Titus flips through the rest of the album. Claude and Charlie listen, mesmerized as he explains the old photos. Soon an hour and half has flown by. Charlie is apologetic, "I'm sorry, Titus, but the time is getting away from us. This is great information, but I have to be back in Sisseton."

Titus closes the album. "It's been my pleasure to show you the photos. I don't get a chance to get them out that much any more."

I'd love to come back and learn more," Claude offers resoundingly.

"Me too." Charlie nods. "But duty calls now."

"Speaking of calls." Claude smiles. "Mind if I use your restroom?"

"Just down the hall." Titus points.

"Thank you." Claude excuses himself and maneuvers down the hall.

Charlie shuffles toward the door and Titus follows. "You keepin' my nephew in line?" Titus jokes.

"Oh, yeah," Charlie assures.

"He's a good boy." Titus nods affirmatively. "That's a shame about that girl. That's his wife's cousin, no?"

"Yeah." Charlie frowns.

"You guys getting it figured out?" Titus questions.

"Working on it." Charlie's frown deepens.

The cat has left its station on the couch and moved to its owner's feet. It circles Titus' legs in a figure-eight. "Old Chompers must be jealous of you guys giving me attention." Titus observes, leaning down to stroke the cat's tail.

"Nice to have some company." Charlie smiles at the cat.

Claude is out of the restroom and at the door. Salutations are exchanged and Claude and Charlie hit the road heading back to Sisseton.

Chapter 16

Danny

Sisseton Public High School

Nat had been watching the clock all morning. He was anxious to get to lunch, and the time had arrived. He is out of his American History class and in the sea of students pushing down the hallway. Lunch time is the only truly free time the students get, sitting by whom they want to, talking without being shushed. It is a critical part of the educational experience in socialization. Nat is excited to talk to Katherine about the homecoming dance. It had barely crossed his mind previously, dances and other social activities, but something in the way Katherine looked and talked when they discussed his going to Webster's homecoming seemed to come over him. For the first time in his life, Nat lets his mind think about having a girlfriend and how that might fit into the basketball side of his life. His conclusion was that it fit. Nat makes it to his locker and puts away his books. The lunchroom is just down the hall, and the din of a hundred voices in the dining facility is overwhelming. "Behind you." Nat hears a voice. It is Katherine, and she's with Danny Warren. The three get in the lunch line together. They make quite the trio. Danny Warren is a senior classmate of Nat's and sticks out like a sore thumb. He is the sole Goth-style follower in the high school. He's a big kid, a little doughy, not a dainty, frail, delicate boy one might associate with his proclivities. Danny has stopped with the white powdered makeup, black lipstick, and eyeliner, but he has kept dying his hair an unnatural jet-black. He dresses in all black everyday. It's a uniform for him, black jeans, black shirt, and a rotation of black jackets. Today his coat is a black leather motorcycle jacket with several buckles.

Nat watches Danny and Katherine interact and converse in the lunch line ahead of him. He can't hear the words, but Danny's effeminate mannerisms could convince anyone that he is actually a girl. Nat smiles to himself as he pictures others looking at the three of them in line. Misfits lumped into a trio he imagines...a Goth, a pretty blonde, and a tall, wiry Indian. It dawns on Nat that Sisseton High School has never singled him out, or any others that he noticed, for ridicule. The kids seem to accept everyone, going along to get along. Another thing that Nat had noticed about kids his age, in general, is that most are fairly lazy, staring at their phones all day. It would be work to actually pick on somebody or make fun of them. Nat's self awareness for his age is rather on the developed side. He doesn't fit the mold of the majority of the teens. He is busting his butt for what he loves, basketball. He doesn't have time to relax like everyone surrounding him seems to. Not a care in the world, that's what almost all of the other students exude.

"Did you talk to him?" Nat whispers to Katherine, as they get their trays and move through the serving line.

"Yes, it's ok," She whispers back.

Nat's body releases its tension he hadn't even realized he'd been holding. Receiving their pigs-in-a-blanket, applesauce, tater-tots, and green beans along with a carton of milk, the kids are on their way to find their table. The lunch room is rather antiseptic. It is just the foyer to the gym. The décor is dominated by a gray tile floor with half the room's wall accommodating the built-in benches and tables for seating the students at lunch. The group passes the built-in furniture for the portable tables and finds an unoccupied half of table. Danny and Katherine sit on one side of the table, and Nat plops his tray down opposite of Katherine. They all dig in; the food is good when you're hungry, and teenagers are always hungry. It's Danny that breaks the silence. "I heard you in line. It's ok, Nat. I'm not upset you're moving in on my girl." Danny meets Nat's eyes with his, and he smiles. His effeminate, lispy speaking voice is something Nat will never get used to.

"I know you two have been friends a long time," Nat acknowledges.

"My first friend...and pretty much my only friend," Danny lisps. He throws one arm over Katherine's shoulder and pulls her close for a quick hug. "Did you know that we met in kindergarten?"

"Really?" Nat questions.

"It's true," Danny continues. "I'm her best, Indian, gay, Goth friend."

"You're Indian?" Nat questions, not sure if he heard correctly.

"Yeah," Danny nods. "You didn't know that?" He laughs and leans across the table in an exaggerated whisper. "Mostly people are surprised and question the 'gay' part of the description."

Nat shrugs. "I just didn't know...about the Indian part. I can kinda guess the other stuff."

Danny laughs loudly, truly entertained. "I like you Nat."

"Where you from?" Nat continues his questions.

"I'm from here," Danny replies between tater-tots. "But I'm an enrolled member of the Flandreau Tribe."

"Hmm," Nat laughs softly.

"What?" Danny questions defensively.

Nat shrugs, "I just never suspected."

"Well, now you know." Danny pops another tater-tot in his mouth. "Don't you worry about your date. Your girl is safe with me."

Chapter 17

Supper Time

LeBeau Residence

Supper time at Charlie's house includes Veronica this evening. It's pork chop night, and Claude has grilled tonight's fare. The click and clank of silverware on plates dominates the dining room as the focus is on the food. "Good job on the pork chops, Grandpa," Nat finally interrupts the quiet.

"Thank you." Claude grins as he shovels a chunk of the other white meat into his mouth.

The pace of eating slows, and Veronica speaks up. "So, you guys all ready for turkey hunting this weekend?"

"Can't wait." Nat nods.

"Ready as I'll ever be," Claude chimes in.

Nat points to the window. "We got the resident flock out here that's practically tame."

Charlie takes a drink from his water. "I wouldn't be so sure. Those birds have a sixth sense when it comes to the hunting season."

The group falls silent again as they eat in earnest. Veronica rekindles the conversation, moving it in a different direction. "How's cross country going?"

Nat shakes his head. "I'm not on the team. I'm not running. I'm just a student manager and working out with them...for basketball."

"Oh," Veronica acknowledges.

"We had a meet over in Britton this week." Nat drinks from his water glass. "And I learned something new."

Nat looks to his uncle. "Found out Uncle Charlie was right; Webster doesn't like Indians."

"What?" Veronica flinches.

"Yeah, Grandpa and Uncle Charlie told me that Indians aren't welcome in Webster, and they're right."

"What happened?" Veronica quizzes.

"One of the girls on the Webster cross country team asked me to their homecoming dance. But...she rescinded. She said she had to make a college visit. Her parents demanded she fit the visit into their schedule."

"You don't believe her?" Veronica continues with the questions.

Claude and Charlie focus on Nat and his story as they continue to eat. "No," Nat proceeds with his retelling of the experience, "You should have seen her dad swoop in and whisk her away from me as quickly as possible. He's a doctor by the way."

"That's too bad." Veronica frowns. "Sad."

Nat waves away the emotions. "It's fine. It's actually worked out better for me. Katherine asked me to go to Sisseton's homecoming dance with her."

"Oh, good!" Veronica cheers.

"Webster's a dump anyways," Claude grumbles. "Nobody needs it."

Charlie grimaces in concern before he speaks. "Some things and some places never change...and never will."

"It's weird," Veronica pauses as she thinks about it, "I have never noticed it or heard that before. Huh."

"How's the paper going?" Nat questions Veronica, turning the tables on her.

"Good!" Veronica replies always excited to talk shop. "You should come by. My new employee, Brad, played college football. You could talk to him and get a preview of college life and what he went through and what you'll be doing soon."

"I'll do that. I'll swing by." Nat chews on a crescent roll. "What stories you workin' on now?"

"The Hopkins girl, of course." Veronica's eyes meet Charlie's. "Anything new, Charlie?"

"No comment," Charlie manages between bites of baked potato without looking up.

Nat looks to Charlie. "Pete, he's on the cross country team, asked me at the meet the other day, about the dead woman. He said there's talk about her murder and those slaughtered antelope. What's that about?"

"You mean the Shadow Dancers?" Claude smirks.

Veronica's eyes widen.

Charlie shoots Claude a dirty look. "Dad," he says with a warning tone.

"What are the Shadow Dancers?" Nat questions.

Veronica's eyes widen further. Charlie shakes his head and continues to eat.

"Nothing much," Claude shrugs. "Just the most powerful of the mystical medicine men on the reservation. Very secretive."

"Yes," Charlie grumbles glaring at his father. "Very secretive because they don't exist." He turns his attention to Veronica. "Shadow Dancers. They are the gremlins of the reservation. Shadow Dancers are what get blamed when something that can't be explained, happens on the rez."

Claude smiles mischievously. "Could be true. There's nothing to disprove it. Like Bigfoot. Just because nobody's found one, doesn't mean they don't exist."

Charlie sets his knife and fork down in a huff. "They don't exist, because they don't exist...never mind. I'm not going to have this conversation again and again."

Claude laughs. "I believe Shadow Dancers exist. If they don't, what killed those pronghorn then?" Claude continues to get under his son's skin.

"Poachers," Charlie says flatly.

"Ah, yes..." Claude holds up his finger. "Shadow Dancers in the form of poachers."

Charlie's eyes roll. Veronica looks back and forth between Claude and Charlie. "Is there anything I can put in my story?"

Everyone is silent. "Nothing?" Veronica questions demonstratively. "Nothing off the record?"

"They are unrelated," Charlie frowns. "Claude and I just had a conversation with a local expert. They are unrelated."

"Who's the expert?" Veronica demands.

"It's Titus Korman. Skip's uncle. Up in Veblen."

"So nothing?" Veronica mumbles quietly.

"I will tell you one thing." Charlie holds up a finger. "One thing I can share. Rodney might get out of jail. Get his daughter."

"Well, that's good." Veronica nods, satisfied.

"We'll see," Charlie grunts. "What's the forecast for Saturday?"

"Nice," Claude enthusiastically provides.

Nat holds up his hand. "We got a cross country meet, so I can't hunt too long in the morning.

Claude and Charlie nod, acknowledging the comment as they continue to eat.

Chapter 18

Opening Day

Opening morning of the fall turkey season starts in the dark. With a light breakfast under their belts, Claude, Nat, and Charlie are on the front porch, shotguns in hand, discussing the final preparations. Charlie's two and a half acre homestead granted by the tribe abuts the farm fields of the neighboring farm and ranch owned and operated by the Hakken Brothers, Pete and Lars. The reservation is a checkerboard of landownership. In the early days of the reservation and before the official reservation boundaries were recognized, homesteaders claimed their one hundred and sixty acres. Until the federal government took over the responsibility of the lands through the Department of Interior's Bureau of Indian Affairs, the trust responsibility to hold the land for the Tribe was a bit adrift. The tide has turned direction in the modern day, with the Sisseton-Wahpeton government buying as much land as it can as it comes up for sale. These efforts have added greatly to the landholdings of the Tribe in the last few years, mostly thanks to the Indian casino revenue.

For Charlie and his crew of hunters, they have permission from their neighbors to hunt the adjacent Hakken property. The Hakken brothers don't hunt much any more and have turned over the exclusive rights to Charlie. It's a mutual benefit as it gives the brothers an eye out in the field to seemingly help dissuade trespassing. Their hunting grounds include the woodlots and the wooded streams and coulees carving up the land around the edges of the cropland. It makes perfect habitat for wildlife, especially the deer and turkey, with cover, water, and food all in the same place.

There is a slight breeze from the north and no moon. The porch light blocks out the stars as Claude shares his plan. "I'm just walking right down here to the coulee. You guys all set?"

"Yeah," Charlie confirms. "Remember, I'm taking Nat downstream. I'll go back on the county road and drop him off at the culvert. If you hear him shoot, be ready." Nat moves down the steps. "I'll be upstream from you about a mile. One of us should be able to get a Tom." Charlie follows Nat to his old Ford pickup.

"Good luck," Claude calls out as he heads toward trees in the dark. He flicks on his headlamp as Charlie fires up the truck and its headlights illuminate the shadowy-eerie-tree-filled coulee ahead of Claude.

Claude hits the edge of the trees and begins the descent down to the bottom of the coulee. He had been scouting the area for his opening day spot for the last two weeks. Ducking and dodging in the tangle of trees, he moves down the slope. Once at the bottom and across the stream he can head just fifty or so yards north and that is where he is going to set up. It is on the edge of a little clearing in the woods, and it seemed like this was the path of the flock he had seen on his several scouting trips. The turkeys fly down from their roosts and trudge through the clearing, avoiding some of the morning dew of the taller grass.

The day's hunt is over before it even begins in earnest for Claude. He trips on a tree root and tumbles down the sloping bank, bouncing into trees. His shotgun is separated from his hands, and his headlamp flies from the top of his head. He comes to rest against a tree. He is dry, hung up in the shrubs, a couple feet short of a cold bath in the stream at the bottom of the coulee. An improbable miracle, his fall is cushioned by the trees, keeping him out of the shallow creek that dribbles and bubbles nearby in the dark. It is only two feet wide and about six inches deep, but the familiar sound of water is the first thing Claude recognizes as he recovers from his fall and the ringing in his ears subsides. He can feel the warm blood trickling into his eye from a gash on his forehead, a result of a tree branch to the noggin. He touches the source of the blood and winces at the sting, both from the flesh wound and the shooting pain in his wrist. He notes his ankle throbbing.

The sky is just now showing the faintest hint of daylight's approach. Claude rights himself, pushing to a knee. Claude's senses are coming back to him. He notes the stream gurgling a few feet away. "At least I didn't fall in the water," he laughs the words out loud.

He gets to his feet with a groan and another laugh. He holds his injured wrist with the opposite hand. He raises both hands to his head and wipes at the blood on his forehead. He steps gingerly, limping on his twisted ankle. "Nothing seems to be broken," he grumbles aloud.

Claude shuffles up the hill carefully, slowly. He zeroes in on the headlamp shining downward into a patch of leaves on the forest floor. Snatching up the headlamp, he tucks his handkerchief over the cut on his head, securing it with the elastic headlamp band. "Where's that stupid gun?" Claude calls out loudly, becoming angrier by the minute at his foolish misstep and tumble.

He grumbles aloud, chastising himself as he makes his way slowly up the bank. In a few minutes he has located his shotgun. He empties the weapon, putting the shells in his pocket. The old Remington 870 shotgun shows the wear and tear of fifty years of hunting. One couldn't tell if the spill put another ding in the wood stock or forearm of the ancient gun. Using the old gun as a crutch, Claude manages to scale the tangle of trees and slope in the darkness that is slowly giving way to the dawn.

A Charlie LeBeau Mystery

Chapter 19

Spirit of '76

The morning hunt concludes, and Nat waits in the shade of the trees near the road where Charlie dropped him off a couple hours earlier. He can't help but grin as he looks down at the large Tom turkey at his feet. As predicted, one of the big Toms had strutted by a half hour ago. The unsuspecting bird met its fate with the roar of Nat's shotgun. Nat strokes the iridescent feathers with the barrel of the shotgun and silently thanks God for the success. The familiar throaty growl of Charlie's old truck draws Nat's attention as it chugs down the gravel road, approaching his position where the county road intersects the coulee. The battery of culverts services only a trickle of water on this warm autumn day but sits ready to move plenty of water from an upstream storm with its configuration of four, forty-eight inch corrugated metal pipes.

Nat reaches down and grabs the feet of the turkey, careful of the long, sharp spurs on its heels. He holds it up high as he emerges from the trees, crosses the bottom of the road ditch and climbs the slope to the road. Charlie reflects the smile of his nephew as he spots the proud young man with his trophy. "You got one!" Charlie calls out from his open window.

"Yup," Nat replies with a grin. "It's a pretty nice one."

"Wow, look at those spurs. Heckuva beard too." Charlie gives a low whistle. "Congratulations."

"Thanks." Nat lifts the bird and tucks it in the bed of the truck behind the cab. He moves to the passenger side of the truck, ejecting the shells from his camouflaged Remington 870 pump shotgun. He gets in the truck. "And you?" Nat questions as Charlie turns the truck around on the gravel road and gets headed back to the house.

"Nada." Charlie twists his mouth in disappointment.

"Did you hear any shooting from Grandpa?" Nat questions.

"Nope," Charlie shakes his head. "Only heard you shoot once. I waited a half hour and thought I'd come and see what you got. I was pretty sure that one shot meant success."

Nat shakes his head, still in a state of disbelief over his luck. "I thought Grandpa would have gotten a shot for sure. That's where those turkeys always are."

"Who knows?" Charlie shrugs. "With this warm weather and wind, maybe those birds are out of their usual pattern."

Charlie steers the truck off the county road down the driveway to his house. It is a beautiful morning, and the wind is a tolerable ten to fifteen miles per hour from the south. It is warm and humid, feeling like rain, and Nat cranes his neck as he looks at the sky through the windshield. "It feels like rain, but there's not even any clouds."

"Yeah, no clouds, but something must be coming with this much humidity." Charlie agrees. He pulls the truck up onto the concrete drive pad and parks.

Nat's door is open, and he is yelling immediately. "Grandpa! Come out and see the one I got!" He moves to the back of the truck, opens the tailgate, and jumps in the truck's bed. Nat touches the ugly, bare skin on the turkey's head. He examines the stringy beard of the bird and smoothes the rest of the feathers. "Charlie, you got your phone? Maybe get a couple pictures for me?"

"Sure." Charlie digs for his phone in his pocket.

The front door finally opens, and Claude emerges onto the porch. His head is wrapped with gauze and a small splotch of blood has soaked through on his forehead. His left wrist is in a makeshift sling from an athletic wrap. He limps across the deck to the railing and peers down on Charlie and Nat. "What'd ya get?" he calls down with a grin.

Nat lowers the bird he is holding as he stares at Claude. Charlie is also staring at his dad. Both look up at the man in stunned silence. Claude cranes his neck to see the turkey, but the pickup truck bed is blocking his view. "Oh, you got a nice Tom. Hold it up, so I can see it better."

"Grandpa," Nat finally speaks, his voice husky in surprise. He lifts the bird unconsciously following Claude's request as he tries to comprehend what he is looking at on the porch. "What happened to you? You look like that Revolutionary War painting. You know that wounded guy playing the drum."

Charlie snorts a laugh, but immediately snaps back to concern for his father. "Are you ok, Dad?" Charlie steps forward and climbs up the stairs to get a better look at his father.

Claude waves away the concerns with his good hand and arm. "I'm fine. I tripped and fell down the bank in the dark. Got a little banged up. Didn't even get a chance to hunt."

Charlie touches the bandage on Claude's head and shakes his head. "Come on, get yourself ready to go with us. I'm taking you to IHS."

"Indian Health Service?" Claude flinches. "I'm fine," he insists.

"Nope," Charlie says matter-of-factly. "You're going to the emergency room. You might need stitches." Charlie's voice changes from his police-persona to concerned family member. His tone hits a higher pitch. "Dad, blood's coming through your bandage." Charlie points to Claude's head. "What about your arm?"

"I'm fine," Claude stubbornly replies as he grimaces while trying to move his arm around as proof of his condition. "Ouch," he whispers, wrist throbbing.

"Listen, Dad, I got to run Nat into town to catch the bus for cross country anyway. You are coming." Charlie points to the door. "Get inside and get ready." Charlie turns to Nat. He points a finger at him and the turkey, "Go gut that thing and hang it behind the shed. Make sure it'll be in the shade for the next couple hours. I'll take care of it when we get back from town."

Nat nods and is down from the truck. He lays out the turkey on the back of the truck and gets a knife from the cab. Charlie yells down to Nat, "Hey, take it down to the tree line and leave the guts there. A fox or a coyote might want a snack." Nat nods as Charlie opens the front door and yells to Claude, "You ready yet?"

Chapter 20

Hospital

Indian Health Service Hospital – Sisseton, South Dakota

With Nat dropped off and on his way to Milbank for the cross country meet, Charlie waits with Claude behind a curtain in the emergency room. Emergency is a relative term in that it had been a half hour since they were brought back from the check-in desk. A nurse has performed a preliminary inspection of the head wound, felt Claude's wrist, looked at his ankle, and taken his vitals, including temperature and blood pressure. After all that the nurse left saying, "The doctor will see you in a few minutes."

After forty minutes, a middle-aged round nurse parts the curtain. "Claude, Charlie, how we doing?" It is Gabby Renville, one of Charlie's high school classmates. She's dressed in pink scrubs and grabs the chart. Her round face is framed by thinning, brown, wavy hair, with streaks of gray hair that appears not to have seen a brush in a while.

"Hi, Gabby," Claude replies. "I guess the triage nurse thought I was going to live."

Gabby smiles. "Claude, you just have to be patient. We only got one doc, and since you're stable, you wait." Her grin widens, and she giggles. "Good news is your vitals seem remarkably fine. The doctor will see you in just a few minutes." She exits drawing the curtain closed.

"Here we go again," Claude groans. "Just a few more minutes." Claude lies back on the examination table on which he's been sitting.

Charlie folds his arms as he sits in a chair against the wall, close to Claude. "Hey, you're a low priority. If you got a bunch of nurses hovering over you, then you got a problem." Charlie's eyes scan the room through the partially open curtain surrounding them. The simple, antiseptic space is partitioned into four bays each with its own curtain. An open space

99

forming an aisle down the middle of the room allows the medical personnel to travel back and forth, and Charlie watches as nurses march in and out of the curtained-off areas.

Claude heaves a sigh as he stares at the ceiling, hands folded across his stomach. "Looks like you'll have to fill my turkey tag. I can't believe this." Claude holds up his damaged wrist. "Probably no way I can shoot a shotgun."

"We'll see," Charlie responds softly as he closes his eyes. "Once they get the x-rays, we'll know what we're dealing with. If it's just a sprain, you can probably get out there...not in the dark though." Charlie opens his eyes and grins at his dad with a chuckle.

Claude laughs, eyes closed now. "Yeah, I better stick to daylight hunts. I sure wish I was out there now, instead of being stuck here."

With the end of Claude's statement, the curtain pulls to one side, and a young nurse pushes a wheelchair forward. "Which of you is Claude?" Charlie points to his dad on the examination table. "Let's go for a ride." The nurse jerks her head toward the chair, her long, black hair streaked with excessive blonde highlights, whips at the motion.

Claude begins to push himself up. "The doctor didn't even see me yet," he protests.

The young nurse in the green scrubs is definitely of Native American heritage. She looks to be her twenties. A long-sleeved, skin-tight Under Armor shirt matches her black hair color. "Just climb aboard; you've been cleared. Gabby consulted with the doc and ordered the x-rays."

The relative calm of the emergency room is shattered by a rush of personnel to the ER receiving doors. The wail of an ambulance siren throws the area into chaos as the shrill warning call echoes down the halls and cuts off. Charlie and Claude look silently on as the emergency room reacts in full response mode. "Excuse me," the young nurse mutters, abandoning the wheelchair and tugging the curtain closed behind her. She rushes away to join a crowd of medical personnel.

Charlie and Claude listen to shouting and what sounds like a herd of footsteps rushing into the room. Charlie moves to the curtain and pulls it back so he and Claude can see. A gurney is wheeled into the emergency room examination area directly across from Claude. A little girl is at the center of attention, an EMT is performing chest compressions astride the girl, and a nurse rhythmically squeezes a respirator bulb over the child's nose and mouth.

"Beverly?" Charlie calls out. He sees an almost unrecognizable woman, her face twisted in shock and horror staggering into the room behind the mass of medical personnel. It is Beverly LeCompte. The woman is lost, in shock. Charlie moves forward. "Is it Denise?"

"On three," an EMT calls out. "One, two, three." The medical team lifts the girl to the examination table, and the gurney is hustled out of the way by a nurse. Charlie grabs hold of the shrinking Beverly, steering her out of the way and enveloping her in his arms.

He knows the little girl on the table being worked on is Denise. He talks soothingly to the woman, trying to turn her away from the mania surrounding the efforts to revive the little girl. "She's not responding," the doctor calls out, his voice rising in frustration.

The first sobs emanate from the woman in Charlie's arms. She reaches toward the girl, but Charlie restrains her, keeping her out of the way of the medical team. He strokes her hair and holds her tightly, trying to provide some comfort. "Do something!" Beverly cries, her voice cracking. The sobs give way to a shriek of hysteria that draws the attention of the medical team for a moment. The doctor looks up and yells pointing to the door, "Get her out of here!"

Chapter 21

Just an Accident

BIA Police Station – Sisseton, South Dakota

Charlie sits slumped in the chair across from Skip's desk, a picture of bad posture. The windowless office is even more somber than usual on this Monday morning. "What happened, Skip?" Charlie speaks painfully. He stares at the ceiling. "Did Beverly talk to you?"

Skip frowns as he spins a pen on the calendar-blotter on his desktop. He seems mesmerized by the rotating pen. "Sunday. Helen and I stopped at her house. She was all doped up on valium and who knows what. She was practically catatonic."

"What did she say?" Charlie's eyes move from the ceiling to his boss as he awaits an answer.

"Just an accident." Skip shrugs, his eyes never moving from the pen he continuously rotates in front of him. "Beverly said she was baking cookies one moment, next thing she knows, she hears a scream and a thump. Denise fell down the stairs."

Charlie's eyes return to the ceiling. It is silent in the room for a minute. The only sound is the pen Skip continues to rotate in front of him. Charlie stares at the ceiling; his eyes closed, hands folded on his mid-section. He mumbles just loud enough for Skip to hear him, "Happy Monday to us."

"I just can't believe this," Skip groans. He slaps the palm of his hand down on the pen, halting its revolutions.

"What time did Agent Brown say he'd be here?" Charlie questions.

Skip starts up the spinning pen again. "He is not going to be here until after lunch. He said he was getting the autopsy report on Cassandra from the state lab, and they wouldn't have it ready until after ten."

"Late afternoon then," Charlie states.

"Yeah," Skip confirms. He looks at his friend slumped in the chair across from him. "I hate to even ask, but how bad was it with Rodney?"

Charlie's head begins to move back and forth slowly, "The worst." Charlie groans as he pulls himself into an upright position in this chair, stretching and rotating his neck and back after sitting in such an awkward position. "The prosecutor dropped the charges, and the judge ordered his immediate release when they heard the news." Charlie's eyes meet Skip's. He shakes his head and continues, "When I told him his little girl was dead, he refused to leave the jail cell. He just slid the barred-door closed and slumped against the wall, easing himself to the floor."

"He accused Beverly, didn't he?" Skip questions.

"Of course," Charlie shrugs. "But, he blamed you and me even more. He told us. He warned us."

"It was an accident." Skip frowns. He holds the pen in his hand ready to spin it again, but for the moment, he holds it still.

Charlie heaves a sigh. "I feel like shit. Four years old. Sickening." Charlie pushes himself up from the chair. "I don't mean to be disrespectful or insubordinate, boss, but I don't believe it was an accident." He moves toward the door.

"Charlie..." Skip calls after his friend.

Charlie holds up his hand as he stands in the doorway ready to exit. "We'll talk more when Agent Brown gets here. Give me a call when he arrives."

"Wait, Charlie." Skip pushes himself from his desk and hustles to the door. Charlie is annoyed, but waits in the doorway. "I wanted to ask you about Claude. Is he ok?"

Charlie manages a weak smile. "Yeah, thanks for asking. He's got chipped bone in his wrist. He's gonna be in a cast for awhile. There goes turkey huntin' for him."

"Oh, that's good." Skip nods. "Well, not good, you know what I mean." He shakes his head trying to explain. "It's good that it wasn't worse."

"He got a couple stitches in his forehead along with a sprained ankle." Charlie's head shakes slowly. "We're just not as young as we think we are."

Skip puts a hand on Charlie's shoulder. "You tell your dad, I'm thinking about him and praying for a speedy recovery."

"Thanks, Skip. I'll be sure to tell him." Charlie pulls away and moves down the hallway.

"I'll give you a buzz when Brown gets here," Skip calls down the hallway.

Charlie waves a hand in acknowledgement as he strides away.

Chapter 22

Archie & Moose

To clear his head, Charlie marches out of Skip's office to his BIA police Tahoe. He hits the streets of Sisseton, cruising the east-west streets first, then up and down the north-south avenues. Everyone he passes raises a friendly hand in a wave. It is a bit of reassurance after the heavy conversation this morning. How much blame should he shoulder for the death of a four year old girl? Charlie's mind cannot block out the look of contempt Rodney had shown when he broke the news. Rodney's expression was an image of a man sequestering himself from society. His pleas for the police to protect his child had fallen helplessly on deaf ears. Rodney is never going to recover; that's the one thing Charlie walked away with this morning.

Charlie is killing a few more minutes as he waits to pick up Veronica for his lunch date. The drive makes him feel better, especially his reception on the street. There isn't anyone he passes so far, that doesn't wave and smile. Little do they know how much their friendliness means to Charlie at this moment, this sunny but dour morning. It is warm again, above the seasonal average, but the winds are shifting to the north and the familiar fall crispness of the air can be felt even as noon approaches. The melancholy tones of Teddy Geiger singing "For You I Will (Confidence)" contribute to the mood. Charlie shoots a disapproving glance to the radio with a frown, but lets the song play.

An open parking space in front of the Roberts County Standard Newspaper office invites Charlie to pull in and park. The door gongs an alert as he enters the office. Veronica is at the far end of the wide open work space. Chad Merriwether, a big, thick-necked man, sits at the desk closest to the door. The twenty-two year old looks more like a boy; with his fine blonde hair and freckled face. He could probably pass for a twelve year old boy if not for the hulking size of his body. "Morning, Charlie," Chad welcomes a smiling Charlie.

Pheasant Country radio plays on the office sound system. Just above the threshold of auditory recognition, Charlie notices Patty Loveless singing "Hurt Me Bad" first, and then the DJ mentions a "noon-time-double-play" and Patty sings again, this time it is "Don't Toss Us Away."

Charlie looks across the room, happy to see Veronica. It is a relief for Charlie to see the love of his life after the gut-wrenching morning. He doesn't look at Chad, instead his eyes remain on Veronica, "Oh, hi, Chad."

"Terrible news on that little girl," Chad says softly. "Any comment from the BIA police for my story?"

Any positive trajectory for Charlie's mood is deflated by the question. "The usual comment." Charlie frowns.

Veronica looks up from her computer as she hears the voices. She smiles, and Charlie is instantly back on track for a better day.

"Right." Chad nods. "No comment then." He scratches and scribbles into a notepad a moment before turning his attention to the computer in front of him.

"I'm gonna take your boss out for lunch. You want us to bring you something?"

Chad opens a drawer and pulls out a clear, plastic zip-lock bag. "No, thanks. I pack my own lunch." He holds up the bag and inside the gallon-sized bag are smaller bags of powders, pills, and energy bars.

"Mmm, looks good," Charlie quips sarcastically. Charlie's attention is tilted back to Veronica. She is on the move, heading toward him as she clutches her purse, fumbling with the clasp as she stuffs her cell phone in the bag. She looks down at Chad as she passes. "I'll be back."

Chad smiles. "Don't worry. I'll hold down the fort."

The door gongs as the couple heads out. Charlie gives a wave as the door closes behind him.

*   *   *

It is just a few minutes drive from downtown Sisseton to the Dakota Connection Restaurant located in the northeast quadrant of Interchange 232 on Interstate 29. The Monday lunch crowd is filtering in for the chicken strip basket, a popular midday meal choice. Three big strips of battered and deep fried breast meat with a generous portion of fries.

Charlie and Veronica are seated and don't need menus. They both choose the special and Cokes without hesitation. Veronica can sense Charlie's tension. He didn't say a word on the drive from the newspaper office to the casino restaurant, and now he's staring up at the back wall. The overhead speakers in the restaurant play a soothing Keith Urban song, "Only You Can Love Me This Way." Veronica speaks with a sigh. "Pretty rough couple weeks for the news headlines."

Charlie's head snaps to meet Veronica's eyes. "Hmmph, did you say something?"

"What's wrong, Charlie?" Veronica pleads. "You're a million miles away. I was just saying that it's been a rough couple weeks."

"I'm sorry." Charlie shakes his head with frown. He rubs his chin. He looks around the restaurant as it continues to fill with hungry people. The din of conversations is getting louder, and Charlie scoots closer to the table, so he can talk quietly to Veronica. "Tell me about it. Depressing. Seems like we get waves of bad things like this on the reservation. A cycle."

Veronica leans in, pleased she finally has Charlie's attention. "They say it happens in threes, you know." Veronica cocks her head and sighs. "When it rains it pours."

Charlie scans the room again; his head shakes as he examines the faces surrounding him. "I'm struggling with it. That little girl." Charlie's eyes are locked with Veronica's, and he unconsciously fiddles with his badge on his shirt, straightening it. "I have this guilt. Rodney warned us. Skip is insisting it was an accident, but he doesn't know. He's got a personal stake involved with his wife's cousin. It's a mess. Beverly was like a sister to Helen. They were raised by their grandmother. She was the maid of honor at the wedding."

Veronica nods. "You've had your doubts since the beginning, at least with Beverly."

"Yeah." Charlie twists his mouth.

"Come on." Veronica smiles. "Let's ditch the work talk and just enjoy lunch." Veronica pulls her silverware from its wrapped napkin, placing the utensils on the table and folding the napkin on her lap. She bends and folds the sticky-note napkin-wrapper as she talks. "You going to get Claude back out turkey hunting this next weekend?"

"Yup." Charlie half-heartedly smiles. "But he'll probably have to just sit with me. He won't be able to hold a shotgun with his cast."

"He's got a cast?" Veronica questions.

"Yeah, he had a chipped bone in his wrist, so they put a cast on it. The recoil of shooting is probably too much anyway, so it's best he doesn't shoot."

"Wow," Veronica breathes the word. "I didn't know it was that serious."

"Stitches in his head, sprained ankle, and the wrist. He'll tough it out."

"Good."

"Pretty lucky." Charlie flinches at the thought of Claude's mishap. "It's scary to me. Parents get old; just can't do what they've always done. It's sad."

"You need to treasure your time together," Veronica whispers the words emotionally.

Charlie blinks as he is taken aback by his insensitivity. "I'm sorry, you're right. Look who I'm talking to, an orphan." Charlie slumps in his chair a bit, embarrassed.

Veronica reaches across the table, extending her hand. Charlie holds out his hand, and she grabs Charlie's hand in hers, "You know who else is an orphan? Nat." She pauses and looks deeply into Charlie's eyes. "And we both have you. We're both very lucky." Charlie forces himself to smile. Veronica shrugs. "It goes both ways though. Claude needs to realize that he can't do everything like he used to."

Charlie leans forward again. "I talked to him about that. I got to get him a cell phone too. What if he woulda lain at the bottom of the coulee all morning?"

"Cell phone. That's a good idea. The problem is, what if he forgets to take it with him? I forget mine sometimes."

The food arrives in plastic baskets lined with red and white checkered paper. Fries overflow the containers and fall to the table as the waitress sets them down. "Mmmm," Veronica hums as she digs into the steaming hot French fries.

They eat for a few moments in silence, enjoying the chicken with dipping sauces: barbeque, sweet and sour, and honey. "Hey, guess what?" Veronica blurts out a little too loudly in her excitement.

Charlie looks around the room. "What?"

Veronica beams with pride. "I have a new high school sports correspondent for the paper!"

"Oh, really? Who?"

"Nat!"

"Good." Charlie nods, satisfactorily.

"Yeah, he's going to do summaries of the cross country meets. Profile team members. Good stuff."

"Wow." Charlie gives a bit of a chuckle of disbelief. "I'm surprised he agreed to do it." He shrugs, "I look forward to reading his stuff." Charlie's brow furrows a bit in concern, "Have you actually read anything of his? Can he write?"

"Yeah." Veronica is offended by the question. "He's good. I told him I needed a writing sample before I could hire him. He wrote an article about the cross country meet up in Britton. It's going in the paper, a little behind schedule, but it was too good to waste." Veronica sighs. "I only wish I had gotten him signed up sooner."

Charlie is still a bit in disbelief, "How did you convince him?"

"You remember the other night at supper? We talked about him coming over to talk to Chad. Well, he did. He was sold on the idea. I'm going to try to persuade him to do the same for the Redmen football games too. Game summaries and player profiles. Readers will love it."

Charlie grins, his mood brightening. "Moose talked him into it?"

"What?" Veronica flinches. "Moose? You mean Chad?"

"Yeah," Charlie laughs. "Moose from the Archie comic books." Charlie's smile turns into a puzzled frown. "Hey, if Chad is Moose, does that make me Archie?" Charlie points at the pretty lady across the table from him and smiles wryly. "Because you are Veronica."

Veronica laughs with a snort. The mirth is cut short by Charlie's ring tone. He looks at the display. "It's Skip." Charlie answers the phone with a push of a button. It's a short conversation. "Hello. Ok. Yeah. About an hour then. See ya." Charlie pushes the end-call button, and stows his phone back in the breast pocket of his uniform opposite of his badge.

"What's up?" Veronica questions between French fries.

Charlie buttons up his pocket. "Agent Brown called. He's in Aberdeen. Should be here in about an hour."

"You going to talk to him about Denise?" Veronica sips from her Diet Coke.

"I'm sure it'll come up. He's bringing the autopsy report on her mom, so I'm guessing we'll have multiple topics to discuss." Charlie's mouth puckers in thought as the somber circumstances come back to his mind. He sips from his Coke and starts on his last chicken strip.

The couple eats for a few moments, each lost in thoughts brought on again by the phone call until a shadow passes over their table and stops. "Hi, Charlie." Courtney German announces her presence.

Charlie looks up from his chicken strip as he chews. He swallows with difficulty, "Oh, hi, Courtney."

Courtney is dressed in a fine, expensive, pant suit with a crisp white shirt and cuff links. She looks a bit out of place with her outfit. She smiles and looks back and forth between Charlie and Veronica. "I just wanted to stop by and check to make sure the food and service were up to your standards."

Charlie sips from his Coke trying to recover from his surprise. "Yes, very good." He wipes at his mouth with his napkin. "Courtney, do you know Veronica? Veronica is my friend, my girlfriend."

Courtney extends her hand, and Veronica shakes it. "Hi." Courtney smiles. "I've seen you around, but we've never been introduced. I'm Courtney German, the business manager out here."

Veronica nods. "Veronica Lewis. I run the newspaper. Pleased to meet you."

Courtney holds up a finger as she remembers. "I think we've talked on the phone. We usually run ads in your paper."

Veronica lights up. "Oh, yes! Definitely!"

Courtney waves both hands, almost like a magician finishing a trick. "Well, let me get out of your way. I just wanted to stop and say 'hi,' so, hi." She places her palms together as if praying and points her hands to Veronica. "Nice to meet you, Veronica."

Courtney walks away, and Veronica stares at her. She shakes her head as her eyes stay trained on the beautiful woman. "Oh, my God, Charlie. You are right. I am jealous. She is stunning."

Charlie smiles and reaches across the table, grabbing Veronica's hand in his. Veronica meets his eyes. "She's ok." Charlie grins. "Don't worry, I'm with you, and you're with me."

Chapter 23

Has a Ring to It

BIA Police Station - Sisseton, South Dakota

FBI Agent Austin Brown stands next to the table in the conference room, twisting from side to side. "Man, that drive is starting to get to me." He stretches one way than the other. "My back."

Charlie, Skip, and Jeremy sit at that table, waiting patiently. "You're gettin' old," Charlie comments with a wink and a smile. "Welcome to the club."

"It only gets worse." Skip frowns a moment, but quickly smiles as he looks at Jeremy who is staring at him with a puzzled look. "Don't worry, Jeremy, you got plenty of time, but your day will come."

Jeremy looks around the room at all the men that are approximately twice his age. He shrugs. "Yeah."

Skip points to the accordion folder on the table next to Agent Brown, "You going to show us the report or we supposed to read your mind?"

"Fine." Brown stops his stretching and reaches for the accordion folder. He releases the elastic band that binds it, but stops as he hears a rap on the open door.

The group looks to the doorway. "Uncle Titus?" Skip questions as he sees the old man peeking around the door frame. "What are you doing here?" He waves the man into the room, and Uncle Titus shuffles forward. "Everyone, this is my Uncle, Titus Korman."

Titus gives a wave as he sets an ancient photo album on the table. "The lady at the desk told me to come on back," Titus says as he flips a thumb in the general direction of the lobby.

Charlie stands and pushes his chair towards the old man. "Here take my chair."

"Thank you," Uncle Titus responds as he sits.

"How did you get here?" Skip questions.

"I hitched." Uncle Titus shrugs.

"Hitched!" Skip's voice rises in concern. "We got to talk." Skip looks around. "Can I talk to my uncle?"

Jeremy stands and Charlie, along with Agent Brown, make a move toward the door. "Hold it!" Uncle Titus orders. "All you guys need to hear what I have to say." He taps a finger on the album in front of him. The men halt and turn back to the table. "I heard about Beverly." Uncle Titus looks at Skip. "I knew right away."

"Knew what?" Skip questions, annoyed.

"It's why I had to get here," Uncle Titus sighs. "It was an emergency, that's why I hitched." Skip starts to point a finger at his uncle. "Put your finger down," Uncle Titus orders.

He flips through the book to a page marked in the photo album. It is a black and white photo, yellowed with age. It is slightly out of focus, but it clearly shows a man hanging from a tree, noose around his neck, head covered, and hands bound behind his back. In the background, completely out of focus, on-lookers surround the hanging tree.

"Whoa," Charlie flinches as he looks over Uncle Titus' shoulder. "Who was it?"

Uncle Titus taps his finger on the page next to the photo. "That was Henry White Clay. You ever heard of him?"

Jeremy speaks up, "White Clay? As in my part of the country, Pine Ridge?"

Uncle Titus nods. "Very good. Henry White Clay was from Pine Ridge. He married into the Bird family...that's Beverly's kin."

"So?" Skip holds up his hands in question. "What is this all about?"

"Well, let me get to it." Uncle Titus looks at the men staring down at the photo. "Anyone have a guess on why they hung this man from this tree?" Titus observes heads shaking. "My father explained to me that his dad, my grandfather, gave him this photo and the story that goes with it. Henry White Clay was just an average guy until one day he sliced off his wife's ears." The men in the room cringe at the story. "Nobody knew why he did it. Justice was swift. The Bird family was well respected, and vigilantes strung him from that tree in a mere matter of hours." Uncle Titus pauses and looks around the room. "Consensus was that Mr. White Clay had gone insane." He pauses again and meets the eyes of each man. "It runs in the family. Beverly is about the same age that it struck Henry White Clay. Something goes wrong with wiring in their head."

Silence blankets the room for several moments. Skip blushes, embarrassed by his Uncle, "Uncle Titus, could you go wait in my office?" Skip points to the door and to the left. "It's right next door." Uncle Titus closes the album and nods as he pushes his chair back and struggles to get to his feet. "I'll be right there, and we'll get you back home. You're not hitch hikin' back home."

Uncle Titus shuffles to the door and gives a wave as he departs. "I'm sorry, guys." Skip forces a weak smile, as he turns his eyes to Agent Brown. "You want to show us the report?"

Agent Brown stands in front of the binder on the table below him, still mesmerized by the old man's blunt conclusions. "Sure." He stretches the binding's elastic band to release the cover and pulls out the report and photos. He spreads the photos out on the table and flips through the report. "It says here, according to the medical examiner, cause of death was massive internal bleeding caused by trauma."

"No surprise there." Skip shrugs. "Pretty much figured that."

Agent Brown continues reading from the report. "Bruising on victim present in layers. Injuries showed different stages of healing with new bruises overlapping old injuries."

Charlie examines the photos one at a time as he listens. He picks up one of the 8 x 10 color photos printed in actual size. He places his fist over the image of what appears to be a bruise in the shape of a fist in order to compare the size of his hand to the photo. He notes his hand is much larger than the photo of the bruise. "Multiple bruises indicate that a weapon," Brown reads from the report, "or possibly an object such as a ring, on the assailants hand, were present."

Charlie freezes as he hears the words. His head snaps towards Agent Brown. The word "ring" echoes in his head. He drops the photo in his hand, stands, and rummages through the photos spread before him on the table. Agent Brown looks up from the report as do the others. "What is it?" Brown questions, observing Charlie frenetically flip through photos, searching for something, anything. "What are you looking for?"

Charlie doesn't look up as he pores over the photos. "You said *ring*, the word *ring*,"

"Yeah." Agent Brown cocks his head.

Charlie locates a photo of a bruise with what appears to be the outline of a fist; individual fingers are identifiable, along with a geometric imprint of where a ring would be worn. He holds up the photo. "There. Here it is." Charlie looks at Skip. "It's Beverly."

Skip flinches and frowns, puzzled. "What do you mean?"

Charlie moves over to where Skip sits at the table. He holds the photo a moment before dropping it in front of Skip. He stabs his index finger on the photo. He taps the area of the photo where the bruising surrounds an explicit geometric shape of a flower. "Beverly wears a large ring, like this. Haley, you know, Rodney's other daughter, she told me that Beverly slapped her on the head, and that ring really hurt."

"That's enough for me." Agent Brown points a finger at Jeremy. "Charlie, Jeremy, you go pick her up."

Skip stands, "Wait a minute, shouldn't I…"

Agent Brown cuts him off with an admonishing palm of his hand, "Stay out of it, Skip."

Skip nods his head slowly as he eases back down into his chair. "Don't worry, Skip." Charlie speaks softly, "it'll be ok."

Chapter 24

Rebound

Sisseton Public High School Gymnasium

Slightly out of place, Danny Warren, in his Goth-induced wardrobe, pure black shirt, pants, socks, and bulky canvas coat, "shoots" basketballs at a basket. He takes one ball at a time, and with the form of someone who has never played basketball in his life, he tosses the balls at the rim. The basketballs carom in different directions, and the empty gym is filled with a cacophony of bouncing balls. Danny doesn't hear his fellow senior classmate, Mike Reidholm, approach from behind. "Larry Turd! You tryin' to play basketball?"

Danny jumps in surprise as he turns to the voice. "I..."

Mike Reidholm is a run-of-the-mill jerk. He stands out from the student body in no special way, but he's a tough guy this afternoon, trying to bully somebody who is different. His brown hair and dark complected skin on a puckered face makes him appear as if he is sucking a lemon. His constant sour expression matches his personality. He's around six feet tall and big enough to play as a sub on the football team, and it's where he should be right now, but his slacker attitude let him take the day off. Cutting through the gym to his vehicle in the parking lot, he crosses paths with an unsuspecting Danny.

Nat appears from the locker room in his basketball gear behind Mike and observes the scene before him. Mike's voice is raised. "What the hell do you think you're doing?" he questions with contempt.

Danny holds up his hand in the direction of Nat, "I..."

Mike cuts him off again. "Freak show, Queer Jordan don't belong in this gym."

"That's enough, Mike," Nat calls out across the gymnasium. He jogs forward, squeaking his shoes and pausing every few steps to wipe them with his hands to make sure they have grip. "This is my rebounder for the day."

Mike's expression of surprise and shock as he turns to face Nat flips to a smile. "Oh, Nat. No problem. Sorry to bother you."

"Don't apologize to me," Nat points to Danny. "Tell Danny you are sorry."

Mike turns to Danny and shrugs. "Sorry, Danny. Just having a little fun teasing."

"Shouldn't you be at football practice? You got a concussion? Too many blows to the head?" Nat questions. "Is that why you are talking shit to my friend?" Nat frowns. "Just get out of here."

Mike's head dips and he puts his hands up in surrender as he backs away. "Sorry, Nat."

He walks to the exit as Nat and Danny watch him disappear in a flash of light from the door opening to the bright sunlight. "You ready to rebound?" Nat smiles.

"Thanks for sticking up for me," Danny says softly.

"What? No problem." Nat shakes his head. "I was just thinking the other day that Sisseton pretty much leaves people to their business, but I guess I was wrong."

"Yeah, welcome to my world. Most of the time people aren't that confrontational, mostly whispers behind my back, but apparently somebody pissed in Mike's cornflakes today, and he wanted to take it out on somebody."

"Classic bully." Nat frowns. "What a cliché. Stand up to him, and he backs down like a scolded puppy."

"The world is never going to change." Danny shrugs. "Some people just don't like other people."

"Life's too short to deal with a lot of bullshit," Nat growls. "That kind of stuff pisses me off."

"Take it easy." Danny smiles cheerfully, "Save that attitude for the other team. Come on. Let's get you some practice." Danny picks up a ball from the rack and bounces it to Nat. He takes a dribble and launches a sixteen-footer that swishes, snapping the net. Danny beams and points to the basket. "I helped you do that. That's an assist, right?"

Nat laughs. "If you say so."

"Thanks, Nat." Danny grabs another ball but holds it at his chest, ready to pass. Nat motions and claps his hands for the ball, but relaxes as he sees Danny's not going to throw it. "I just wanted to say thanks for calling me your friend. You didn't have to do that, especially in front of Mike."

Nat sighs and grins. "Let's not get all sentimental here. Anybody that helps me rebound for my shooting drills is my friend. You are quickly falling behind on my friends list by not passing me the ball."

Danny laughs and throws the ball. Nat catches it, dribbles, and banks an eight-footer off the backboard. "All right then." Nat claps his hands. "Let me see if I can hit twenty five free throws in a row. Then we'll try some threes." Nat smiles wryly at Danny. "If you're lucky, I'll give you some shooting lessons before we wrap things up."

Danny is all smiles, enjoying his work. He shakes his head as he grabs another ball off the rack and flips it to Nat heading to the free throw line.

Chapter 25

Resistance

Beverly LeCompte Residence – Sisseton, South Dakota

It is less than a three minute drive from the police station to Beverly's house. Four blocks off Main, on the north side of Cherry Street, Jeremy and Charlie stand on Beverly's porch. The house is in the older part of town, probably built in the 1950's, but it is in an excellent state of repair. The detached two car garage sits west of the house a few yards. In between the house and the garage, a large patio area with a built-in field stone grill/smoker as a centerpiece, is neatly arranged with outdoor furniture. The neatly kept grass is the perfect shade of green. The two men look up and down the house, noting the two story home with a basement is probably about 500 square feet per floor. Charlie holds up a finger of caution toward Jeremy as he knocks on the new front door. The bright red door stands out against the white painted house with black trim. "Just stay near the door," Charlie warns. "I'll do the talking."

Jeremy's eyebrows arch as he looks around the neighborhood and up and down the street. "Is there anybody even home?" He flips his hand toward the driveway; his voice is husky, questioning, "You'd think that with all that happened, there'd be relatives crawling all over the place, providing support."

Charlie nods in agreement, his own suspicions aroused. "You're right." Hands on his hips, Charlie takes in the rest of the neighborhood. No one is around. No cars move on the street. The wind rustles the turning leaves on the tall ash tree in the middle of the front yard. Charlie notes the tree is likely forty-five feet tall, thirty years old at least. The neighborhood is full of similar trees. This is the well established section of Sisseton, filled with the middle class families of the community. Charlie pushes the doorbell, and the men can hear the muffled "ding-dong" chime through the door.

The policemen look at each other and wait quietly on the small covered porch facing the street. Charlie presses the button again. Finally, Charlie hears the faint voice from inside, "Come in! Door's open!" The muted shout is from Beverly, and Charlie reaches for the door knob. He gives a nod to Jeremy and pushes the door inside, entering the house.

The smell of fresh-baked cookies, rolls, and banana bread fill the warm house. The open floor plan of the home allows Charlie and Jeremy to see Beverly busily moving about in the kitchen. The front door opens to the living room with a large flat screen TV, flanked by a couch and chair. A small dining area with a wooden table and chairs separates the living room and kitchen. The counter top between the dining room and kitchen overflows with baked items. Charlie moves forward into the dining area, hands on his hips. Beverly bustles around the kitchen. "Hi, Beverly," Charlie speaks firmly with little emotion. He looks over his shoulder at Jeremy posted at the door just inside the entry way. Jeremy stands on a piece of linoleum, his arms crossed. The living room and dining area are fully carpeted. At the front door a small area about three feet by four feet of smooth flooring is in place to accommodate the dirty, snowy boots of the winter months. On each side of Jeremy there are large, healthy plants in tall planters. One is a bushy spider plant with numerous offshoots hanging to the floor. The other large plant is some exotic aloe vera plant, grotesquely large, it's succulent, barbed, triangular leaves ready to defend itself. Charlie notes to himself that Jeremy looks like an ancient Roman palace guard surrounded by the greenery. "We need to talk to you," Charlie speaks firmly as Beverly bangs pans into the sink.

"Go ahead and talk," Beverly replies as she runs the kitchen faucet, wiping down the pans with a dish rag.

Charlie moves toward the kitchen even with the counter. The kitchen is a u-shape, fridge and stove on one side with the sink against the wall facing the street and a window to look through as one would wash dishes. The rest of the kitchen is counter space with cupboards and dishwasher underneath. "Actually, we need to talk down at the station." Charlie leans against the counter.

"Why? We can just talk here. I'm really busy." Beverly flashes a pained smile. She rinses her hands and wipes them on her apron around her waist. She sets the pans on top of the stove and adjusts the oven controls. "I'm making more rolls, and I have two funerals I'm preparing for, if you didn't know." Beverly lays out round clumps of bread dough on the pan and sets it aside.

"Is anybody else here, Beverly, to help you?" Charlie questions.

"It's just me," Beverly snaps the words. "If you don't mind, I'm trying to get things done." She rinses her hands, wipes them on the damp apron and moves to her next task, washing celery and carrots.

"It'd be better if we just went back to the station to talk," Charlie repeats his request.

Beverly places the vegetables on a towel and pats them down, wiping her hands on her apron again. "What's this about?" She reluctantly shakes her head as she pulls a small paring knife from the drawer and begins slicing the top, leafy portions off the celery.

"It's about Cassie." Charlie grunts the words as he straightens, removing his hand from the counter. The counter between the kitchen and dining area is lined with stools on one side to provide an eating area; the other side is the brightly lit kitchen area where Beverly works diligently cutting veggies.

Beverly focuses her attention on the carrots in front of her. "I'm busy," she replies brusquely. "I don't want to talk about Cassie. I'm preparing for a funeral. Two funerals." Beverly works the knife in her hand slicing carrots length-wise. "I have relish trays to prepare." She waves the knife across her baked goods. "Can't you see all the work I'm doing here?"

"I'm sorry, Beverly, you have to come with us. We have to take you to the station and have you answer some questions. Can we call somebody to come and take over for you?" Charlie questions.

"I don't want to go." The argument continues.

"It's not a request, Beverly." Charlie sighs. "I'm running out of patience here."

"What?" Beverly scoffs. "You goin' to arrest me?"

Charlie holds up a steadying hand. "Look, I know Skip's wife is your cousin, and out of respect, I'm trying to be patient. But the time has come for you to go with me to the station." Charlie heaves a deep breath that turns into a sigh. "Please, come with me."

"No!" Beverly is defiant.

"All right," Charlie shakes his head with a shrug. "Put your hands behind your back." He steps forward casually. In a flash Beverly slashes Charlie's arm with the knife in her hand. She continues to attack Charlie, driving the small blade into his abdomen. He staggers back in surprise. The knife remains lodged in Charlie's Kevlar vest as he breaks away from

Beverly, crashing into the wall behind him. His left hand quickly covers the bloody gash on his arm. He looks down in shock at the handle of the knife jutting from middle of his body.

Jeremy, posted at the ready near the front door, reacts like a cat bounding across the room. Leaping, he flies onto the counter, sliding across the smooth surface sending vegetables, breads, rolls, and cookies flying. He smashes into Beverly, sending both of them into the refrigerator that rocks unsteadily for a moment before settling back to its position. He makes quick work of handcuffing the stunned, groaning woman. He stands, finds a towel, and hands it to Charlie, while keeping his boot on Beverly's back, holding her down, flat on the ground. "You ok, Boss?" Jeremy questions. "I'll radio for help."

"No. No," Charlie pipes in, recovering his senses. "Gol dang it. I let my guard down. Thanks for jumping in." Charlie is in disbelief as he looks at the prisoner on the floor. The pathetic handcuffed woman moans. Charlie gathers his wits. He looks at his arm, blood soaking into the towel. "I hope you learned from my mistake about...about getting too casual. I'm lucky."

"Whoa!" Jeremy shouts and points at the knife sticking out of Charlie's chest. "I'm calling the ambulance!" Jeremy cues the mic attached to the shoulder flap of his uniform.

"No!" Charlie calls out. "It didn't get me. It's stuck in my vest." Charlie wrenches the plastic handle of the knife and it snaps off.

"Let me call it in," Jeremy insists.

"No." Charlie pulls the towel tightly around his arm, the fabric saturating with his blood. "Veronica listens to the police scanner. She'll flip if we have an officer down call."

Jeremy reluctantly nods, conceding the point. His hand drops off his shoulder-mounted mic.

"Come on then." Jeremy steps down on the woman's back, and she grunts, "I'll get you to the hospital.

Charlie nods. He bends down to help lift their prisoner, but he pauses, looking down at his arm with the towel. He makes eye contact with Jeremy, "I better just meet you in the car." Charlie moves toward the front door.

Jeremy's mouth forms into a partial grin. "Yeah, I got 'er." He lifts the groaning woman to her feet. "I'm sorry, Ms. LeCompte. I had to protect my partner." Jeremy steers Beverly out the front door. "You're in real trouble. Resisting arrest. Assaulting an officer. Assault with a deadly weapon. Oh, boy."

Chapter 26

Lucky

Jeremy is behind the wheel of Charlie's BIA police Tahoe with Beverly cuffed in the back, squirming. The young officer pulls into the ambulance bay at the Indian Health Service Hospital, where the emergency room entrance is quiet this weekday afternoon. Charlie exits the vehicle pressing firmly on the towel over the wound. He has some pain now, the adrenaline having worn off. He closes the vehicle door and speaks to Jeremy through the rolled down window. "Remember what I told you now. Book her and lock her up. Don't let Agent Brown start talking to her without me." He looks towards the emergency room doors a moment, but turns back to Jeremy. "And make sure Skip stays out of this. Can't have him contaminate things with his family status."

"You want me to come back and get ya?" Jeremy questions.

Charlie shakes his head. "No, I'll call Veronica to let her know what's going on. She can come and get me."

"Good luck with that phone call." Jeremy grins.

Charlie nods and slaps the door of the vehicle, indicating to Jeremy he can leave. "Thanks again, Jeremy." Charlie holds up his arms, still putting pressure on the wound and awkwardly waving to his protégé. "See you later."

Jeremy points a finger. "You call me if you need anything." His words are more of an order than a casual statement, his concern for Charlie showing through. He steps on the accelerator and pulls away. Charlie waves again clumsily.

*　*　*

Inside the emergency room, past the automatic, sliding-glass, entrance doors, Charlie approaches the desk. The waiting area is empty, bathed in the tune of overhead speakers playing a rocking-Muzak version of Joan Jett and The Blackhearts' cover of Tommy James & the Shondells version of "Crimson and Clover."

"Excuse me," Charlie says softly.

A bored nurse in scrubs sitting behind the counter thumbing through a magazine looks up. "Yes?" She sees the uniformed man with a blood stained towel draped on his arm, and she leaps into action. "Oh, my God! Are you ok, Officer?" Out from behind the counter she springs, grabbing Charlie's arm and elevating it above his heart. "Jackie! We have an injured police officer out here! Help!"

Seemingly from nowhere, three nurses are suddenly present, one holding his arm above his head, one pushing him down into a wheelchair, and one by his side as he's wheeled into the examination room. It's Jackie Knight that is beside him as he is transported from the lobby to the actual emergency room. Jackie is about fifty years old, her long black hair has plenty of gray streaking to her shoulders. Her round frame bounces as she keeps up with the pace the short distance to the exam table. "Not good, Charlie, not good," she whispers. "Exam number two," she orders as the head nurse. Her brightly colored, flower-patterned shirt-top billows as she hustles alongside Charlie.

In the exam room, Charlie climbs from the wheelchair to the examination table where he lays down on the uncomfortable paper-covered, adjustable slab. His arm is extended straight up and the small drips of blood run down his arm to his shoulder. "Let's get a blood pressure cuff on him to slow some of the bleeding," Jackie orders. "Get rid of the towel and get a bandage on it. Quickly!" she orders the other nurse.

From behind a curtain on the other side of the emergency room, a curious young doctor in a white coat over blue scrubs emerges and makes his way to Charlie's side. "What do we got?" he questions looking to Jackie. The young doctor sports a crew cut hairstyle and heavy dark-rimmed glasses. Charlie looks at the young, hipster of a man and thinks this guy appears to have just fallen out of the 1950's.

"Doctor Murray, this is Police Sergeant Charlie LeBeau. He's got a laceration on his forearm. He's stable."

"Thanks, Jackie." The doctor grabs the chart. He points over his shoulder and cringes a bit. "Could you go tell the mom with the toddler that I'll be right back."

"Sure," Jackie nods and confidently strides across the room to the closed curtain.

Doctor Murray nods to Charlie. "Just a little respiratory distress in the little boy. They can wait. Let's see what we got here." He washes his hands and dons a pair of latex gloves. He plops down on a wheeled stool and rolls close to Charlie. He removes the gauze padding. "Yup, definitely a laceration." The doctor smiles. "What happened?"

The doctor continues to probe the wound, looking it over carefully. He dabs at the continuous trickle of blood. Charlie shakes his head, "I guess I was a little too comfortable with a suspect. Dropped my guard."

"Well, you'll live," the doctor looks and smiles at Charlie. "Looks pretty superficial. No muscle or tendon damage. You're pretty lucky."

"Yeah, lucky." Charlie repeats as he plays back the scenario in his head. He reaches down to his torso and feels the torn shirt. He delicately touches the blade of the knife still embedded in his Kevlar vest. "Definitely lucky," he mutters.

The doctor stands up from the stool and backs away to the waste container, removing the bloody gloves and dropping them in the receptacle. "I'll let Jackie get the wound cleaned out and the sutures prepped. I'll get you some good and tight stitches, minimal scar. Be right back." Doctor Murray nods to Charlie and Jackie, who has returned to Charlie's side. He smiles assuredly as he heads back across the room to the curtain with the toddler behind it.

"Hi, Jackie," Charlie says with a smile. "It's starting to hurt pretty good now."

Jackie works busily setting a tray into place with all the suture materials in line, ready for use. She rips open a packet of gauze saturated with antiseptic and swabs Charlie's arm. The wound oozes blood. "Ouch," Charlie flinches.

Jackie shakes her head. "Tch, tch, tch," she clucks. "Not good, Charlie."

"I know." Charlie frowns. "I made a mistake. Can't make mistakes in either of our lines of work. People get hurt. People die."

The nurse pauses for a moment and locks eyes with Charlie. Her head nods ever so slightly, and she returns to her work, cleaning the wound. Charlie moves his free hand to his shirt pocket. "You mind if I make a phone call while you do that?"

"You callin' Veronica?"

"Yeah." Charlie frowns.

"Please, by all means, call her." Jackie beams. "I want to hear her yelling at you."

Charlie manages a weak smile. He meekly shrinks back on the table as he scrolls through his phone contacts. He flinches again as Jackie pushes the gauze into the wound. Charlie presses the button on his phone, dialing Veronica. Jackie shakes her head.

Charlie speaks softly into the phone. "Hi. First of all, I'm fine."

The shrill, tinny response of the cell phone's ear speaker is plain as day to Jackie. She snickers and continues to shake her head. "I'm fine. I'm fine. There was an incident. I am at the IHS hospital. I have to get some stitches." A similar, shrill, tinny-blast comes through the tiny speaker of the phone as Charlie holds it away from his ear as he cringes. "I know. I know. A suspect cut me as I was trying to bring her in for questioning." Charlie moves the phone away from his ear as screeches emanate from the phone. "No. Don't rush down here. I do need a ride, but they haven't even started the stitches." Charlie is finally able to hold the phone normally to his ear. "Ok. Love you too. See you in a bit." Charlie ends the call.

Jackie flashes a toothy smile, "That seemed to go well."

Charlie snorts a laugh. "I'm not sure how you define 'well,' but I'm pretty sure that wasn't it."

Charlie tucks the phone back into his breast pocket and his hand slides over the slice in his shirt. "Jackie." He meets the nurse's eyes. "Do you happen to have pliers and a plastic bag?"

"What do you need that for?" the nurse questions with narrowing eyes.

"I have to collect some evidence." Charlie frowns as he unbuttons his shirt, revealing a chunk of silver protruding, but lying flatly in the seam of his protective vest.

"Is that the blade of the knife that got you?" Jackie questions, already knowing the answer.

"Yeah, do you have something to yank it out of there?"

"Sure," she smiles and stands. "I'll be right back. Just hold this gauze down on your arm for a moment."

Jackie digs through a drawer in a cabinet against the wall between two curtains directly across the area where the toddler is being treated. She closes the drawer, and turns back to Charlie, and begins walking back to him. She holds a needle noise pliers and a clear plastic bag. "Success!" she claims with a smile.

"Thanks." Charlie grins as he reaches for the tool.

"I'll do it." Jackie pulls the pliers back as if shielding it from the policeman.

"Fine."

Jackie sits on the roller stool and slides next to Charlie. "Here we go." She parts Charlie's shirt and clamps the tool on to the silver hunk of steel. "There we are, come out of there," she grunts. The blade is freed from the clutches of the vest, and she bags it the heavy duty bag. "I'll put this in your file to keep it out of the way for now. Don't forget to take it with you." She taps his stomach. "Looks like you'll need a new vest. This one's surely compromised now."

Charlie laughs. "Yeah, we'll see if Skip can squeeze it into the budget."

Jackie joins in the laugh.

Chapter 27

Booked

BIA Police Station – Sisseton, South Dakota

Jeremy enters the police station via the rear entrance. From the first step out of the back of the Tahoe the resistance is on. It's a battle as Jeremy struggles to lead Beverly down the hallway of the police station. The woman is fighting, thrashing, and trying to break free from the grip of the officer every step of the way. She stoops forward, as Jeremy leverages her arms trying to subdue her, but she tries to dig her heels into the slick tile floor to no avail. Jeremy shakes his head at the frothing woman. "Ma'am, please. You are only making things worse."

This comment elicits an ear-piercing scream from Beverly, the shriek echoing through the building. The commotion brings Agent Brown and Skip out of the conference room and into the main hallway. The two men can see the silhouettes of Jeremy and Beverly jerkily proceeding down the hall towards them. Jeremy points a finger at Skip. "Agent Brown, can you make sure Skip stays away, and by the way, can you help me get her downstairs to the jail?"

FBI Agent Brown steps forward and grabs Beverly's arm. She thrashes, turning her head in an attempt to bite the man. Brown puts pressure on her shoulder and her head drops. He looks to Skip and waves his hand to shoo him away. "Skip, out." Brown's command reverberates through the hallway as if he is chastising a puppy. Skip begrudgingly nods and hustles down the hall to his office.

"Skip!" Beverly calls out as the captain moves away. "Make them stop, Skip! Help! I didn't do anything!" Skip disappears around the corner, and there is a noticeable drop in Beverly's resistance to the men pulling her to the elevator.

The elevator ride down is silent, but as soon as the doors open, revealing a dingy basement with jail cells lining the walls, the fight is on. Agent Brown and Jeremy pick up the woman and carry her to her cell, sliding the door closed, cuffs clamped tightly to her wrists. Jeremy is breathing heavily after the struggle to carry the battling woman to the cell. Between gulps of air he manages to instruct Beverly, "You calm down and maybe we'll get those cuffs off you."

Agent Brown is bent over, hands on his knees. He looks to Jeremy. "Why are you here by yourself? Where the hell is Charlie?"

"He's at the hospital," Jeremy replies, hands on his hips recovering.

"Hospital?" Agent Brown shouts the word, and it echoes in the basement. "What happened?"

Jeremy throws a thumb in the direction of Beverly, gasping for breath and still raging in her cell. "This woman is crazy. She sliced Charlie's arm with a knife," Jeremy shakes his head in disgust.

"Is he all right?" Brown questions, straightening in concern.

"Probably gonna need a couple stitches."

"Sheesh," Brown shakes his head, looking at the woman. "I never heard a call on the radio."

Jeremy shakes out his arms after the workout of restraining the woman. "Charlie wouldn't let me call it in. Veronica listens to the police scanner."

Agent Brown nods, tilting his head towards Beverly. "Did you read her rights to her?"

"No, not yet," Jeremy breathes deeply. "Charlie told me to book her, but said he wanted us to wait to talk to her. Wait 'til he gets back."

Brown nods. "I think that'll work out perfectly. It'll give her a chance to calm down. You gonna go pick him up?"

Jeremy's head shakes. "No, he's calling Veronica to tell her what happened, and she'll drop him off."

"Yikes!" Agent Brown grins, and it turns to a chuckle. "He's gonna get an earful from Veronica if he hasn't already." His head nods. "We'll wait. Get her in the system. She's not going anywhere soon. Felony assault on a peace officer for starters. That'll keep her put for a while."

*   *   *

The silence on the ride from the hospital back to the police station was worse for Charlie than any loud argument he could have imagined. Veronica stared straight ahead as she steered her old car down South

Dakota Highway 10, her face expressionless. The conversation had consisted of three words between the couple to this point. "Are you okay?" Veronica asked.

"Yes," Charlie had responded.

Now at the station parking lot Veronica put the car in park, waiting for Charlie to exit. Charlie lingers in the passenger seat. "I'm sorry," Charlie whispers.

"Do you even know why I'm angry?" Veronica turns and meets Charlie's eyes.

Charlie shakes his head. "Because I got careless and got hurt."

"No!" Veronica raises her voice. Charlie can't help but relax, knowing this is what he expected. "You didn't call for help on the radio, and I know why. You were too scared of my reaction to follow your own protocols!" Charlie raises his hand but is cut off as Veronica continues, "It is scary. You working as a policeman...I find myself thinking about what might happen at all hours of the day. It's maddening. It just pops into my head, wondering if you are ok. I stay busy enough, my mind occupied with work, but it always comes back...are you ok?" Veronica's eyes well with tears. "It's your job, I get it. But, that doesn't make it any easier." She sighs haltingly, on the verge of breaking down. "Please..."

Charlie leans from his passenger seat, but is restrained by the seat belt. He releases the clasp and is able to scoot to Veronica's side and envelop her in his arms. "You're right," Charlie whispers. "I promise...I'll do better."

He pulls away and looks into Veronica's eyes. She nods acknowledgement and kisses him. "We'll be ok," she smiles weakly. She pulls him close and hugs him. "You better get in there. I'm sure they're wondering where you are."

Charlie nods and slides his way to the door, opening it. "Yeah. I'll talk to you later. Love you." Charlie leans down and smiles, locking eyes once again with Veronica.

"Don't work too long. Get some rest," Veronica orders.

"Don't worry." Charlie nods and waves. "Love you."

"Love you," Veronica replies. The car door closes, and Charlie walks away with a wave as he looks back to his love.

Chapter 28

In Front of the Glass

BIA Police Interrogation Room 1 – Sisseton, South Dakota

Beverly sits with one hand handcuffed to the metal table in the sterile interior room. The table is bolted to the floor. The chair she sits on is a cold, metal, straight-backed chair. Nothing could make the room look more like a penal institution. The dark-gray, cement-block walls provide a claustrophobic feeling. Beverly stares at her wrist chained to the welded loop. She pulls on the handcuff, in a steady beat as if she thinks she might break free or wear down the cold steel clasp. Her respiration has returned to normal, a far cry from her caged-animal-like gasps she bellowed as she fought the officer that had brought her from her cell ten minutes ago.

Charlie, Skip, Agent Brown, and Jeremy observe the woman from the other side of the mirrored glass. They watch her rhythmically pull on her handcuffed wrist fixed to the table. Skip's face cringes as he shakes his head. "Something is wrong with her. She's had a mental breakdown or something. Look at her!" His voice rises, and he sweeps his hand toward the glass.

"Ya think?" The sarcasm dripping from Agent Brown's voice eases some of the tension in the crowded observation room. Brown emits a sigh. "She's refused a lawyer five times. She's insisting that we have the wrong person."

Jeremy mumbles, arms folded, "Yeah, wrong person. She has no idea who *she* is. That's my guess. How would she know any person?"

"We're probably going to catch hell from all legal sides, given her state. I know they're gonna say she was in no condition to even be questioned without a lawyer present." Brown frowns. "But, we got to talk to her."

Brown shakes his head and turns to Charlie, who is staring at the woman. A look of pity is painted on his face as he rubs the bandage on his arm. The agent turns to Skip. "You should excuse yourself. Just get out of the building. We don't want this to somehow be looked at as tainted...this interview and everything else."

Skip's head bobs up and down, almost imperceptibly. His shock and disbelief at seeing his wife's cousin has left him visibly shaken, "Yeah," he manages to whisper the word. He looks at Jeremy. "Make sure you get the recording equipment turned on. No mistakes."

"Aye, aye, Boss." Jeremy nods.

"I'll go in first and talk to her." Brown unclasps the accordion folder he holds and thumbs through a couple photos. He opens the door of the observation room, and Skip exits in front of him with a wave. The captain trudges a few steps down the hall. "I'll be back. I got to run Uncle Titus back to Veblen. Can't have him hitchhikin' all over the country."

He sticks his thumb in the air, and Agent Brown nods. Skip shuffles out the back door of the station to the parking lot. Brown watches him disappear behind the closing door of the building before entering the interrogation room.

*　　*　　*

Brown enters the interrogation room and closes the door gently behind him. He remains standing, back against the door, hands behind him. He grips the folder in his hands, the binder is shielded from the woman's view by his body. He leans against the door casually. His voice is calm and soothing as he begins to speak, "Miss LeCompte, I am Federal Bureau of Investigation Officer, Special Agent Brown. I know you have been asked several times now, but are you sure you don't want a lawyer?"

Beverly is calm now. She looks up at the tall man standing near the door. He seems exceptionally tall to her from her seated position. She smiles and replies as if in normal, everyday conversation. "Why would I need a lawyer? There seems to be some confusion. We'll get things cleared up, and I'll be on my way." She shakes her head, her hair flops with the response. "I have a lot of work to do. Two funerals you know?" She pulls on the cuff attached to the table, exaggerating her disgust with the restraint by a wave of her hand.

"I am sorry, Beverly." Agent Brown frowns as he looks down on the pitiful woman. Beverly is disheveled and tired. Her hair is mussed; her make up is smudged and smeared. Dark circles under her eyes are no longer covered by concealer. She can sense the look from the agent, and she pulls the fingers of her free hand through her tangled hair. "Beverly," Brown continues, "it's not that simple. You attacked a police officer. You cut him. With a knife." Agent Brown's head dips, hoping to get some sort of acknowledgement from the woman.

"No," Beverly flinches at the accusation, leaning back in her chair in disbelief. "Why would I do something like that?" She is genuinely confused, and Agent Brown's posture dips in disappointment. He realizes he is dealing with a genuinely mentally ill woman.

Brown pushes away from the wall, hands still clasped behind his back. He looks to the mirrored glass, envisioning Jeremy and Charlie behind it, wondering if they have arrived at the same conclusion as he has. This woman is sick. He paces along the wall with the door, careful not to obstruct the view of the observers behind the glass. "Beverly," Brown sighs her name, "did you ever argue with your daughter?" The agent's words are spoken slowly, soothingly.

Beverly's head cocks. "Of course. What mother doesn't have disagreements with her daughter?" Her tone is incredulous. She smiles with a melancholy sigh. Her lip trembles, but the sigh transitions to a laugh, a hearty laugh. The agent is taken aback. He looks to the observation glass, noting the mood swing. Beverly chuckles, amused by the question, which she repeats, laughing the words, "Did I ever argue with my daughter?" She shakes her head with incredulity.

"What did you argue about?" Agent Brown inquires softly.

"Well," Beverly's tone flips like a switch to angry. "First of all, her choice in men." Beverly's brow lowers, her face pinches in anger. She snaps her words, "She had a drug problem."

Beverly's emotions well up in the form of tears now, streaming from her eyes, rolling down her cheeks unchecked, and dripping to the table. There are no sobs as this manic switch of emotion washes over her. "I begged her to get help. I threatened her. I tried to bribe her. She would hang out with *Rodney*, the loser. Cassie had the gall to bring him to *my* house. A drug dealer! I had expressly forbid him from being there." Beverly grits her teeth, eyes narrowing. "Him and his drugs. He killed her! Maybe not directly, but with his drugs. He pushed her over the edge. Now my beautiful baby...both beautiful babies are gone. My granddaughter. He killed her too, just as if he had put a gun to her head." Beverly stares into the mirror. Her hands tremble, but her voice is steady. "That poor bastard child. Her brain was affected by those drugs." Beverly turns her head to Brown and looks with pleading eyes. "My baby, I told her not to run in the house. She couldn't understand." Beverly's voice cracks as she looks in the mirror. "My poor baby, Denise. She falls right down the stairs, and now I have nobody. Nothing!"

Brown sees the look of bewilderment on her face. He remains silent as he watches the woman. She looks at her wrist as if noticing the handcuffs for the first time. Her body sways as she trains her eyes on her own image in the mirror. Tears continue to flow freely from her eyes. Finally, Agent Brown breaks his silence, his voice restrained, almost a whisper, "I know this is difficult, but I have to ask you some more questions, about Cassie. Are you ok? You think you can answer them?" Beverly nods. "Did you ever fight with your daughter?"

"Yes." Beverly is annoyed. "I already told you. We argued. All the time."

"Did you ever physically fight?" Agent Brown holds a fist in the air. "Hitting her with your fists? Did she hit you?"

Beverly sobs now. The wails combine with a steady flow of tears. She buries her head in her hands, elbows planted on the table. Her hands make their way to her snarled hair. She stares at the table, and tears pool in two puddles off her cheeks. "I had to hit her," she speaks, her voice muffled, directed down toward the table. "She made me hit her. She wouldn't listen!"

Agent Brown steps forward, extracting three photos from the folder in his hand and spinning them onto the table next to her elbow. The actual-sized photos of Cassie's abdomen are riddled with bruises. A photo of her left breast clearly shows a defined impression of a geometric image that blends into the areola surrounding the nipple.

Beverly turns her attention to the photos, blanching as she sees the bare torso and breast. "What is this? This is sick!"

"Those are photos of the bruises you left on your daughter's body," Agent Brown states matter-of-factly. Beverly flinches, not understanding the statement. She pushes away the pictures in disgust. Her head shakes in disbelief. Agent Brown continues, "You see that bruise right there?" Agent Brown pokes his finger down on the photo of the breast. He slides the picture across the table with his finger, right under Beverly's face. She has returned her elbows to the table and rests her head in both of her hands. Brown taps on the photo. He moves his finger from the photo and taps her ring finger on her right hand. "You see that photo? That's the ring you are wearing on your right hand." Beverly pulls her hands from head. She feels the ring on her right hand with her left. She twists it on her finger. "You beat your daughter to death," Brown makes the statement flatly.

"No. No. No," Beverly snaps the words in anger, pausing after each one. Beverly sweeps the photos off the table. She tries to stand, but the handcuff deters her effort and she sits, pointing a finger at Brown. "Yes, I hit her, but she left and took her daughter that night. I threw her out of my house." Her words are tipped with venom now; her ever changing range of emotion has settled upon rage. "I told her to never come back. She walked out of my house alive, and that was that." Brown stares at Beverly for a moment. He shifts his gaze to the mirror, looking at her reflection instead. Beverly grunts the words, "The next time I saw my daughter, she was dead...at the funeral home." The anger is supplanted by cries and wails.

"We're done talking, Beverly," Brown states quietly. "You killed your daughter." Brown gathers the photos scattered on floor. Beverly watches, puzzled her situation. Her cries still echo in the room. Brown returns the photos to his folder. "You are going to need a lawyer." He looks to the mirror and taps on the door, waiting to be let out of the interrogation room.

Chapter 29

Behind the Glass

Jeremy lets Agent Brown out of the secured interrogation room, and the two rejoin Charlie in the observation room. It's a solemn group. They stand in silence observing the murder suspect...a middle-aged lady, Beverly LeCompte, sitting, handcuffed to a table in a dank room, under the harshest of fluorescent light. She appears to have shrunk before their eyes, a tiny lady, still fascinated by the fact that she is chained to a table. They watch her look around the room, seemingly bewildered by her situation. Agent Brown puts his hands on his hips and shakes his head as he stares through the mirrored glass at the suspect. "God damn. She's going to have a mental deficiency defense if I've ever seen one."

"Have you?" Charlie questions. "Have you ever seen anything like this?"

Agent Brown's head moves from side to side, exaggerating his confirmation that he had never seen this before. "Nope. She hit every emotion imaginable in about a two minute span there. Something's going on up there." He points to his head. "Or, more likely, not going on."

"It's not real to her." Charlie breathes a heavy sigh. "Titus was right; that's got to be a version of insanity."

Jeremy nods enthusiastically. "This is the first time I've observed mental illness up close. I'll tell you what." He throws a thumb towards the direction of Beverly. "That is *scary!*"

The men return to silently watching the woman on the other side of the glass. She attempts to run her fingers through her hair, but the handcuffed wrist makes it extremely awkward to comb her hands symmetrically through her tousled hair. She scrunches closer to the table making her look even smaller, diminishing before their eyes. Agent Brown sighs as he stares unblinking through the glass. "How do you guys do it? How can you live here? The reservation? It's depressing?" Brown flips a disgusted hand in the general direction of the woman behind the glass. "How many families out there are just like this?" He sighs again. "I don't know if I can keep doing this, and I don't even live here." His voice trails off quietly, softly.

Charlie's lips pout as he shakes his head. "I don't think the reservation is any different than the rest of the country. I think of it as a small scale model, a concentrated example of what goes on around the rest of the country...and world."

"But, still..." Agent Brown speaks softly. "I don't know if I want to do this anymore."

Charlie shrugs. "What else would you do?" He chuckles a bit uncomfortably, "This is what we do. We're cops." He points a finger at Beverly. "We are here to try to limit the damage people like her wreak on the rest of the population." He shrugs again. "We dropped the ball on this one. We are a little late in total prevention, but we limited the damage. We stopped her." Charlie redirects his attention from the woman to the agent. "So, what else would you do?"

Agent Brown takes a deep breath. "I don't know, but the first thing I'm gonna do is go home and hug my wife and kids and tell them I love them. Then my wife and I are going to talk about the future."

Charlie manages a smile. "It's good to have options."

Jeremy interjects, "I'm definitely going to have to visit my grandma and thank her."

Agent Brown and Charlie nod approvingly. Agent Brown eyes the two BIA police officers in front of him. "That's some good police work, guys. I'll definitely be letting my bosses know about what you've done. They'll talk to the higher-ups in D.C." Brown extends his hand and shake's Jeremy's hand and then Charlie's. He holds Charlie's grip and nods to Charlie's bandaged forearm. "Is your arm ok?"

Charlie glances at his wrapped wound. "I'm fine."

Brown still clutches Charlie's hand. "You didn't answer my question. How do you deal with it, Charlie? How do you live here?"

Charlie shrugs. "This is my life."

"You're a saint, Charlie," Agent Brown declares, releasing Charlie's hand. "We'll be sending the U.S. Marshalls for Beverly. I'll be talking to the U.S. Attorney. It's not going to be pretty."

Jeremy moves to the door. "If it's all right, I'm going to take her back to lock-up."

Brown nods enthusiastically, "Yeah, thanks, Jeremy. No sense in making her just sit there. You got her?"

Jeremy cocks his head. "Yup, she's calmed down now."

Jeremy disappears from the observation room and reappears on the other side of the glass. The men watch Jeremy uncuff Beverly from the table. "God, Charlie," Agent Brown mumbles. "I'm serious. I don't know if I can take much more of this. I think she killed her granddaughter, too."

"She's sick," Charlie replies softly.

They both watch Jeremy through the glass as he stands Beverly up and handcuffs her hands behind her back. She offers no resistance. Her demeanor is subdued; she is in a trance-like state. Jeremy glances toward the mirror and gives a nod to the men behind the glass as he leads Beverly out of the room.

Agent Brown continues his diatribe against the state of society. "All this shit," Brown grumbles. "That priest and the kids before. Now this, another kid. Man, I think I've had my fill. I'm standing in that room," Brown says as he points his finger at the glass pane, "with a crazy woman, thinking, 'What the hell am I doing here?' It just doesn't seem like it can be real."

Charlie snorts a laugh of disbelief, "What would you do? Go ride a desk in D.C.? You'd go crazy." Charlie's facial expression is one of pure disbelief. "You and me, we're out here on the front lines, trying to make it better...safer. That's who we are." Charlie places a comforting hand on Brown's tense shoulder. "That's what we do." Charlie squeezes the man's shoulder and lets it go.

"I'm already going crazy." Brown frowns. "I'll talk it over with Jeanie. We've had an on-going debate about what I should do. We'll talk. I got less than five years left. I could ride it out in some bureaucratic capacity. Maybe be a trainer at the Academy. Teach. This shit wears on you, Charlie."

Charlie shrugs. He is seeing the FBI agent differently. For the first time, he sees Agent Brown as just Austin. The man. The father. The husband. Charlie stands silently, his head nodding almost imperceptibly. "You're a lot tougher than me, Charlie," Agent Brown speaks the words slowly, softly.

Charlie reaches out again and puts his hand back on the agent's shoulder. "Don't do anything rash. Go home. Talk to Jeanie. Maybe you just need a break. A sabbatical." Charlie grins. "I like workin' with ya. I'd miss you if you left."

"Same here." Brown smiles.

Charlie shakes Brown's shoulder. "Go. Get out of here now, and you'll be home before it's dark."

Chapter 30

Take a Ride

Skip drives west on South Dakota Highway 10, his Uncle Titus in the passenger seat next to him in the BIA police Tahoe. "Can you go up through Sica Hollow?" Titus inquires. "It'll be beautiful right now."

"Sure, Uncle." Skip is glad to accommodate the old man. "But you gotta promise me you won't hitchhike anymore. It's just not safe."

"You're so paranoid." Titus waves a hand at Skip. "This is the reservation. I'm an old man. Nobody's gonna do nothing to me."

"Times have changed, Uncle," Skip rebuts. "You gotta be careful nowadays."

They hang a right and head north on Roberts County Road 6. "Fine," Uncle Titus concedes. "I'll just call you when I need a ride." He grins mischievously.

"I'll be there," Skip confirms.

Seven miles of cornfields turning brown and drying in the fall weather, along with scattered stands of wheat stubble pass by the windows. A couple miles west and a jog back south brings the men to Sica Hollow State Park. The heavily forested acreage set aside by the State of South Dakota houses the warm colors of red, yellow, and orange, an artist's palette of turning leaves.

Sica Hollow is known as a sacred place for the natives. Sica, pronounced See-cha, is Lakota for bad, the "bad hollow." The myth is that the springs along the Coteau des Prairies hill side that ooze a reddish, tinted mud and water during some rain events is blood. The area was forbidden to the Lakota; reserved as a supernatural refuge for spirits. Science has shown that mineral deposits, particularly iron, produces the murky, blood-red, seepage trickling down the hillside. It is a beautiful place from any standpoint.

The Tahoe is enveloped by the canopy of the trees overhanging the winding paved road up the side of the Coteau. Skip slowly steers the vehicle up and up the hillside, enjoying the bursting fall colors. A few leaves rain down here and there, forced from the trees by a gentle breeze on this sunny afternoon. Skip has to brake. "Whoa, check it out, Uncle, turkeys."

A line of turkeys marching single file along the narrow road are frightened by the vehicle and quickly step into the trees. "I see 'em." Uncle Titus points a finger and points to the trees. "There they go."

Skip chuckles. "In the State Park they are pretty brave. The huntin' season is on, and here they are, out in plain sight in the middle of the day."

At the top of the Coteau the pavement gives way to gravel, and the Tahoe makes its way to BIA Route 10 and heads north towards Veblen. The pastures on the top of the Coteau are dotted with sloughs and ponds, each body of water teaming with ducks, some with Canada geese. Most of the pastures have been chewed down to a lawn-like height by livestock fattening up for the winter. The short grass is green, thriving in the cool season, the warm season grasses fading to the brown and tan colors of fall.

Gravel ticks and tings under the vehicle, driven by Skip at a leisurely pace. The men enjoy the scenery in silence. "I like that Charlie LeBeau," Uncle Titus remarks apropos of nothing. "He really seems to care about people."

"He's a good guy. Good police," Skip concurs.

"You're right." Uncle Titus frowns. "I won't hitch anymore, but I do need to talk to Charlie. Maybe he can come visit me?"

"Regarding what?" Skip's face scrunches questioningly.

"It's about those poached antelope. The Seeking Water. He'll know." Titus nods.

With the Veblen skyline in view, Skip turns to a sensitive subject he'd been waiting to discuss, knowing that if the conversation went sour, he didn't want to spend any extra time in the vehicle with his sulking uncle. "Uncle," Skip begins, "have you thought about moving to Sisseton? You know, to be closer to family...if you need help?"

"To tell you the truth, Skip," Titus' lips pucker a moment, "I have. I've been thinking about it a lot." Skip is caught off guard by this response, and he glances over at his passenger multiple times, but does not speak. "I think," Titus continues, "let's talk more about it next fall. You can look into some arrangements, but let's just wait on it...for a year."

Skip smiles. Titus smiles. Both men are satisfied that the conversation was broached. Both men are comfortable leaving the discussion on a positive note, for future debate. Skip reaches for the FM radio volume and turns up the music, it's Hunter Hayes singing "Wanted."

A Charlie LeBeau Mystery

Chapter 31

Webster

Charlie LeBeau Residence

Claude rests on the couch watching TV with his ankle elevated. He looks up from the newspaper he reads as he hears a vehicle pull into the driveway and the engine shut off. He ponders for a moment who it might be. He hears the vehicle door close and after a pause, steps coming up the stairs. The door opens and Charlie pushes his way into the living room. Claude flinches, "What are you doing home early?" Claude sees the bandage on Charlie's arm as soon as he asks the question, but Charlie raises his wrapped up limb anyway. "What happened to you?"

Charlie looks at his wound. "You know that Cassandra Hopkins case?" Claude nods. "Well, we were in the process of taking her mother in for questioning, and she, Beverly LeCompte, sliced my arm with a knife."

"You ok?"

"Never better. Five stitches." Charlie pushes on the bandage with his hand.

"Workman's comp and some convalescent leave I bet." Claude grins.

Charlie moves to the couch and flops down. "Hardly. I screwed up. Let my guard down on a little old lady, and this is what happens." He holds up his arm. "I'll probably have to take some remedial training."

Claude holds up his wrist displaying his cast. "Looks like we're both on the disabled list for awhile."

"Yeah," Charlie sighs as he eyes the television. "I asked the doctor, and he told me I better not shoot a shotgun for a week. Recoil might affect the stitches."

"We'll get Nat out there to fill the turkey tags. He's the only one to get one so far." Claude nods his head satisfied.

The men watch the TV as Tony Kornheiser and Mike Wilbon argue sports on ESPNs' *Pardon the Interruption*. "Hmmph," Charlie scoffs. "Wilbon always going on and on about the Bears. The Bears stink! Vikings will dominate them this season." Charlie eyes his father. "Where's Nat this afternoon? Cross country meet?"

"Yeah, he's over in Webster."

"Oh, lucky him," Charlie remarks sarcastically. "What are you doing tomorrow?"

"No plans."

Charlie sighs. "We should go get you a cell phone. Maybe get one for Nat. It's about time I started keeping better track of you two."

"Sounds good," Claude affirms. "Update our communication technology."

"Problem is," Charlie points out, "you gotta remember to have it with you." Claude nods in agreement. "I worry. I was thinking about how you fell down the coulee on the turkey opener. What if you weren't able to get yourself back to the house, and you had laid there for a couple hours? Scary."

"I hate to admit it, but you're right," Claude concedes.

The men watch another sports story as Kornheiser and Wilbon argue back and forth. "What do you think for supper?" Claude questions.

"I don't know," Charlie shrugs. "I was thinking the casino. Maybe I'll give Veronica a call."

"Sounds like a plan." Claude returns his attention to the newspaper, and Charlie settles deeper into the couch, closing his eyes for a minute and listening to the talking heads argue about sports on the television.

*   *   *

The bus trip from Sisseton to Webster is about an hour. It winds through the heart of Coteau des Prairies, up and down the hills and past potholes, lakes, and sloughs of every shape and size as far as the eye can see. The drive meanders west on South Dakota Highway 10, then south at Lake City on South Dakota Highway 25. The leisurely autumn drive takes them through Eden and Roslyn, two fading rural towns along the way through rolling country and into Webster. The cross country meet is scheduled at the Webster Golf Course located right in town. It is a perfect day for a race. The cool season grasses on the links course are lush and green, enjoying the perfect growing conditions of fall. The girls' run is about to commence, and Nat crowds the course route near spray painted markings about a quarter mile from the starting line. He's ready to cheer on Katherine and the other Sisseton Redmen runners. The gunshot cracks, and the race begins. The crowded field of runners is a jumble of legs and elbows. From his vantage point down the course a short distance from the starting line, Nat watches as a clump of runners go to the ground in a chain reaction. "Katherine!" he calls out as all of the runners, but one return to their feet. Katherine writhes in pain on the carpet of lush grass blanketing the fairway. She holds her ankle, eyes tightly closed, as she rolls back and forth. Nat reaches his friend amongst a gathering crowd of spectators surrounding her.

"It's my ankle. I rolled it over pretty good," she grimaces. She meets Nat's eyes for a moment as he kneels next to her. Katherine squeezes her eyes shut, tightly closing them as tears stream from both corners of her eyes.

"I'm here; you'll be ok," Nat comforts the girl with a soothing voice. "Let's get your shoe and sock off before it swells." Nat pulls on her shoe, and Katherine cries out in pain.

"Hold on," Nat comforts. "I got a cold pack in my kit." Nat rummages through his backpack, extracting a blue plastic bag. He punches the cold pack and massages it, mixing the chemicals inside. It is immediately cold, and he places it on Katherine's ankle. "How's that?" Nat questions with an insecure grin.

"It's definitely cold," Katherine whimpers, still squeezing tears from her eyes as she holds them tightly closed.

"I got an elastic wrap to hold it in place. Just hold on." Nat tries to be as reassuring as possible.

The gathering crowd of concerned on-lookers encircling Nat and Katherine parts, and Doctor Kelly Van Wyck emerges. "Excuse me," he repeats over and over as he separates from the spectators. He frees himself from the encompassing group. "Before you wrap it," the doctor says as he kneels down, "let me take a look."

Nat backs off and the doctor grips Katherine's ankle as she winces. He squeezes and kneads her ankle. He looks to Nat. "Impressive response, Nat. Go ahead and wrap it." He looks to Katherine and gives a shake of his head. Katherine reluctantly removes her arm from covering her eyes and opens them as she whimpers.

"You're going to need an x-ray to rule out any fracture. There could always be a hairline break. I'm sorry." Doctor Van Wyck grimaces. "Keep that pack on until you can get some real ice on it. Limit that swelling," he commands with a nod. "You'll recover that much quicker, barring no broken bones." The doctor looks for the runners on the course and spots the pack topping the hill in the distance. "I gotta go see how my daughter's doing. Take care," he calls out with a wave of his hand as he jogs away.

"How bad is it?" Nat questions. "You gonna live?"

As Katherine props herself up on an elbow and manages a smile. "That cold pack is easing some of the pain. Still throbs though. I got some ibuprofen in my purse that might help." Katherine shakes her head. "I can't believe he complimented you. Wow. Maybe he's changing his mind about *you people*."

Katherine smiles and snickers, causing Nat to chuckle. "Not likely," Nat scoffs. "Come on, I'll give you a piggy-back ride back to the camp. We should be able to see the finish from there."

Nat helps Katherine to her feet. She hops on her good leg to position herself and climb on Nat's back. "Here," Nat reaches down and grabs his backpack. "Carry this."

Nat rumbles across the fairway with Katherine holding on, arms tightly gripped around his neck, draping over his chest. "Looks like I won't be able to rebound for your shooting session when we get back tonight," Katherine comments into Nat's ear.

"That's ok," Nat grunts as he carries the load on his back.

"I know what." Katherine slaps her hand on Nat's chest repeatedly, "I'll call Danny. He's helped you before; he knows what to do. What do you think?"

"Sure," Nat responds with a grunt. "Call him."

"Soon as we're back to camp." Katherine whacks Nat on his behind with her free hand, "Hee-yaw, mule," she yells out playfully.

"I'm glad you're feeling better," Nat groans.

"I'm just making lemonade out of lemons," Katherine quips, feeling Nat's strength beneath her.

Chapter 32

Not-So-Able Bodied

Nat shovels bite after bite of Frosted Flakes cereal into his mouth as he sits at the dining room table reading his history text book. The long afternoon at the cross country meet has left him half-starved and crunched for time to study. His study guide worksheet is half filled out, and he thumbs through his book as he eats. The front door opens, and Claude enters followed by Charlie. "Hey," Nat calls across the room. "What do you know about history?"

Claude laughs. "You're gonna have to be more specific."

"U.S. History," Nat elaborates.

"Well," Claude clears his throat and begins to sing Sam Cooke, *"Don't know much about history. Don't know much biology..."* Claude continues to hum the tune.

"Oh, please," Nat mumbles. Claude and Charlie approach the table, and Nat notices the bandage on Charlie's arm. "What happened to you?"

"Nothing." Charlie rubs his hand over his injured arm. "What happened to you? I thought we'd be picking you up from the gym after your shoot around?"

Nat frowns. "Katherine turned her ankle and couldn't rebound for me, so she just gave me a ride home."

"I'm sorry to hear that," Claude sighs. "How bad was she hurt?"

"Bad enough to put her out of the meet. Barely a couple hundred yards after the start, she stepped wrong and took down half the pack with her." Nat gives a bit of a chuckle as he recalls the event. "Fortunately for the rest of the pack, she was the only one who couldn't continue. I think she'll be fine. They're going to get precautionary x-rays tomorrow."

"I see." Charlie reaches forward, setting a Styrofoam container on the table. "Brought you a burger and fries, but I can see you're eating."

"Mmm," Nat's eyes widen. "Don't mind if I do." He scoops the last few bites of cereal into his mouth and pushes the bowl of milk to the side. Digging into the container he takes a bite of the burger and chews, one by one, he adds fries to his mouth, as he works on the bite of burger. Talking with his mouth full, he mumbles and points to his arm then to Charlie's. "Vuf ampen too-mur-yarm?"

"Don't talk with your mouth full." Charlie chastises. "But, if you're wondering about my arm, I got cut during an arrest. Five stitches. I'm fine."

Nat nods. "So, you need somebody to rebound?" Claude questions. "I'd do it, but I'm kinda banged up."

Nat manages to swallow. "Both of ya on the disabled list. How we gonna get our turkeys, or I should say, how are you guys gonna get your turkeys, since I already got mine?" Nat laughs mockingly.

"Looks like it's up to you." Claude shrugs. "I can't shoot with the bone trying to heal."

Charlie shakes his head. "Same here, at least for a week. Stitches need some time. Looks like the pressure is going to be on you to fill our tags."

Nat takes another hefty bite of the burger. "Ahfv khan vanild eht," he mumbles with his mouth full as he waves away the comment.

"Stop talking with your mouth full. You're gonna choke," Charlie warns again. He points a finger toward Claude and another toward Nat. "By the way, you're each getting a phone tomorrow. Nothing fancy, but we need it for stuff like tonight. You could have saved us a trip to the school." Charlie looks at his dad. "And your grandpa here, if he takes another spill, he can call somebody."

Nat swallows and clearly calls out, "I want an iPhone."

"I already said *nothing fancy*," Charlie cautions and wags a finger at a grinning Nat.

"Just had to ask," Nat chuckles. "Any phone will do for me." Nat wolfs down the rest of his burger. He holds his finger in the air as if he wants to say something, but after being corrected twice for talking with his mouth full, he chews as Claude and Charlie wait in suspense. He chews and chews, finally swallowing. "Speaking of phones." Nat stands and goes to the counter and returns with a piece of paper. "Some guy called and wanted to talk to you. Titus. He said you'd know what it's about." Nat hands over the note to Charlie.

"Hmmm," Charlie grunts. "It's kinda late. I'll call him tomorrow."

Claude holds up his hands questioningly. "Care to enlighten us?"

"It's about those pronghorn that where poached."

Claude and Nat nod knowingly. Nat sits back at the table and pulls his history book close. "He call to confess?"

Charlie can't help but laugh. "Not quite. Not sure what an eighty-year old man would do with a pronghorn."

"Watch it." Claude points a finger at Charlie. "I'm getting close to that number."

Charlie rolls his eyes as he looks at Nat. "I rest my case, exhibit 'A' Mr. Turkey hunter."

Claude holds up a finger and is about to wag it at his son, but freezes with a laugh as he eyes the cast on his arm. "You got me there."

Nat grabs his bowl of leftover cereal milk and gulps it down with a finishing, "Ah." He looks to Charlie and Claude and then to his worksheet. "Back to history, what would you say was the final factor that lead to the Civil War?"

Claude scratches his chin. "I'd probably say the shooting and cannon-fire, where was it, Fort Sumter?"

"So helpful," Nat complains sarcastically.

"Hey." Charlie defends his father. "He was there; he would know." Charlie laughs heartily and slaps his knee, enjoying his own joke.

"Hilarious," Claude groans as it is his turn to roll his eyes. "You're going to have to phone a friend."

Nat snaps his fingers and points a finger his grandpa. "Thanks for reminding me. I gotta call Danny and see if he can rebound for me while Katherine recovers." Nat springs from his chair and grabs the cordless phone.

"Hey." Claude whispers. "Ask him about the Civil War. I think I'm right."

"Grandpa." Nat whines. "Yes, the Civil War started at Fort Sumter, but the question is more about what final political thing happened."

"Bah." Claude waves a hand. "I'm not into politics."

Nat digs through the papers in a folder. "I know I wrote his number down." Nat is distracted with his search, and Charlie and Claude get the hint. The conversation is over.

Chapter 33

Shoot Around

Sisseton Redmen High School Gym

The official activities of the day are over, and students and coaches are clearing the gymnasium as the unofficial activity begins for Nat. It's his routine. For Nat, he has a minimum requirement of five hundred shots a day that he first charts and then completes a thorough, systematic analysis of the results. Behind the art of shooting a basketball, there is quite a bit of math and science. Every spot of the floor, well virtually every spot on the floor broken down into five-foot diameter areas on and within the three point line, has a success rate by a percentage associated with it. All his hand written notes from each shooting session are transcribed on a weekly basis. Computer graphics, charts, and whatever venue of data you would want to see shows up, or could be shown, on a computer screen reflecting Nat's strengths and weaknesses on the floor when it comes to shooting.

The ball rack squeaks as Nat rolls it onto the court. On the far side of the gym he sees Danny. "Hey, man, glad you could help me," he calls out, his voice echoing in the gym. Nat dribbles a ball as he pushes the rack to his starting spot.

"No problem." Danny doffs his leather sport coat revealing a customized white T-shirt emblazoned with a hand-drawn likeness of the Sisseton Redmen logo. Lettering encircling the design spells out Sisseton High School bordering the top of the image and Redmen bent around the bottom.

"Nice shirt," Nat comments. "Is that your own work?"

"You better believe it." Danny tugs on his shirt stretching it for easier viewing.

"Let me guess." Nat stops dribbling and palms the basketball. "You didn't sign Eve Long Spear's petition to change our name and mascot?"

Danny's face contorts at Nat's question. "Hell no! She has no idea what she's talking about. As an Indian, excuse me, Native American, I think it's cool that we get to represent our team."

"Yeah," Nat nods, starting to dribble the ball again. He lets go of the ball rack and sets his pen and clipboard down. He bounces the ball rapidly circling each leg in a figure eight and then reversing the direction after two completed revolutions.

Danny continues to rant about the mascot as Nat dribbles. "And another thing, what's the deal with the Washington Redskins logo for the NFL? There seems to be a bunch of people with too much time on their hands protesting all kinds of penny-ante stuff, when there are real problems." Danny continues to get worked up as he watches Nat. "Eve...and the others, they just want attention. They couldn't care less about what the topic is. As long as it seems controversial and they might get publicity, there they are, front and center for the photo op and any TV camera." Danny's blood boils and he yells, "Aarrgh! Why did you get me started?"

Nat bounces the ball head high and rights himself, stretching his back, he catches the ball at his waist. "Me? All I did was ask you if made that shirt?"

"You asked about the petition?" Danny hollers.

"Oh, yeah." Nat smiles sheepishly.

Danny holds up his hands and looks skyward as if seeking divine intervention. "Why?" he whispers.

"If you're done prayin,' let's get started," Nat quips mockingly. "Rack's got ten balls on it, I'm gonna shoot 50 racks." Nat holds his hand over the rack, and then points to the clipboard. "As important as shooting, I need to keep track of the results. You're gonna have to help me keep track of misses and makes, as well as rebound."

"How long does it take?" Danny nods in understanding.

"Should be an hour, hour ten if you're a good rebounder." Nat smiles. "And I'm hittin' 'em."

"Sounds good; bring it on!" Danny claps his hands. "Can we play some music?"

"Sure."

Danny hooks his phone to the ball rack with its Velcro case. He presses a button on the phone and a 1980's R&B song, "Rock Steady" by the Whispers plays. "You like this music?" Nat questions, wincing at the tinny sound of the electronic percussion.

Danny chuckles, "C'mon, man. It's classic! It grows on ya."

It's a good workout for both boys as they plow through rack after rack of balls. Danny is up to the task and almost on the dot, the five hundred shots are complete and recorded in an hour. Both are breathing hard and sweating. "Well, that was a little more than I expected," Danny pants as he bends and puts his hands on his knees.

"You did good," Nat remarks. "Let's see if I can hit twenty free throws in a row before we call it good.

"Ok," Danny concurs. He grabs the ball rack and moves into position underneath the basket. His phone squeaks out another 80's R&B tune, "Don't Disturb This Groove" by The System.

Nat drains the first ten shots without a word. Only the music plays. Roger sings "I Wanna Be Your Man" another 1980s' R&B tune with early electronic auto-tuning. Nat nods along to the tune. "Hey, you're right. I kinda like this music."

"Told ya," Danny states matter-of-factly.

Nat swishes three more free throws. He repositions himself on the line and looks at his rebounder. "How would you like come turkey huntin' with me?" Nat questions out of the blue.

"What?" Danny flinches. "Did you say turkey hunting?"

"Yeah."

"You want me...to go turkey hunting...with you?" Danny repeats the question emphasizing each word.

"Sure" Nat shrugs holding the ball. "You ever hunted anything before?"

"No!" Danny forcefully laughs the word.

Nat shrugs, dribbles the ball, and shoots, sinking the free throw. Danny rebounds the ball and returns it to Nat. "Come on, I need some help. Both my uncle and my grandpa are hurt and can't go with. Get back to your native roots." Nat points at Danny's t-shirt. "I'll show you how to shoot a gun."

"I don't know." Danny frowns.

"You don't have to shoot, in fact." Nat shoots another free throw and leans, trying to put some body English on the ball bouncing on the rim. It finally falls through the rim. "I was thinking maybe you could just walk the coulee, and maybe, just maybe...chase 'em to me."

"That, I can do." Danny holds up a finger. "I can definitely go for a walk in the woods...as long as I don't get lost."

Nat laughs. "Don't worry. We won't lose ya. Just follow the stream downhill, not too tough. We'll take care of you."

Nat gets the ball back and shoots. The ball swishes through the net. He finishes this twenty in a row to end the evening shoot around. "That's it then?" Danny questions.

"Nope, one more thing." Nat nods his head to the ball rack. "Grab a ball. This is the fun part."

"What?" Danny questions suspiciously

"Follow me!" Nat orders dribbling to half court. "Half-court-shot-shootout!"

Nat dribbles to the half court line and launches a high arcing shot that swishes through, snapping the net like a whip

"Holy cow!" Danny exclaims. "How did you do that?"

"Come on, I'll teach you," Nat instructs.

With all the patience of an experienced professor, Nat goes over each step of dribbling toward the half court line to get momentum, lining up the same knee and elbow as if shooting a layup, finally the aiming point, and follow through.

Ten tries later, Danny sinks a half court shot and is ecstatic.

Chapter 34

Phone Tag

For Charlie it is the first time in awhile that he feels things have gotten back to normal. An open murder investigation will do that. It will put you on edge. No matter how much you try to set it aside during "non-working" hours; it's still always in the back of your mind. Will somebody else die because you can't solve the case? It had played out that way in Cassandra's death. Denise had died as well, and that is still eating at Charlie. He knew in his gut something was amiss with Beverly, but he could not overcome what seems so obvious after the fact. Here in his BIA police Tahoe, Charlie is finding things right with the world. He drives north on South Dakota Highway 127 heading to Veblen. This autumn morning is as crisp as any day so far this fall. The streaks of the wipers still mark the morning dew across the windshield. The sky is the perfect blue unencumbered by clouds. There's hardly a vehicle on the highways as Charlie makes a turn to the west, heading down South Dakota Highway 106 through Claire City finally rolling onto South Dakota Highway 25 and into Veblen. The first hints of the approaching cold weather are foretold in the yellow light of the morning as the earth tilts on its axis away from the sun, changing the angle the sunlight travels through the atmosphere. The yellow light of the coming winter puts life in a different perspective, a melancholy, thought-provoking perspective. Pheasant Country plays on the radio. Jimmy Wayne warbles his painful, plaintive wish of "Stay Gone."

Charlie's morning errand is an appointment with Titus Korman. Charlie had returned the old man's call and was assured by Titus that the case of the poached pronghorn was solved. Titus was to present the evidence, and Charlie could work with the game wardens to arrest the culprit. Titus had demanded Charlie come in person to receive the proof, and Charlie was obliged to visit.

Grobe's gas and grocery bustles with early morning activity as Charlie passes. On the south side of Veblen in the government housing area, there is no activity. Charlie parks on the street in front of Titus' house. He is right on the mark, precisely 9:30 A.M., the agreed upon appointment time. He exits the truck and the inside door of the house opens a moment later as Charlie approaches. Through the storm door, he can see the old man wave him inside. Bounding up the steps and pulling the door open, he enters the home. The powerful scent of coffee greets his nostrils producing an involuntary smile across Charlie's face. He spies the black and white cat, Chompers, tipped over on its side enjoying a sliver of sunlight on the carpet in front of an east facing window. "Coffee?" Titus calls out from the kitchen.

"Sure," Charlie replies.

"Have a seat."

Charlie sits at the kitchen table, and Titus places a mug of coffee in front of him. "Cream? Sugar?" Titus questions.

"No, thank you." Charlie hoists the mug towards Titus. "Thanks," he remarks with a sip of the steaming hot beverage.

"Right on time." Titus sits across from Charlie with his own mug of black coffee.

Charlie begins, "So, what's this evidence you are holding hostage?"

The question is interrupted by a buzz of Charlie's phone in his breast pocket. He digs the phone out and sees the caller is Claude. He holds up a hand to Titus and receives a nod of permission from the old man. He answers, "Dad? What is it?"

From the other end of the phone, Claude responds, "Nothing, just checking the phone."

Charlie can sense the childlike glee in his father's voice, a kid with a new toy. He can't help but smile. "Ok, Dad, I'm busy. I'll give you a call later and make sure your phone is working. Bye."

Charlie shakes his head and smiles at the grinning old gentleman across the table. "I'm sorry. My dad. I just got him a new cell phone, and he's making sure it's working." Charlie tucks the phone back in his pocket. "So, what you got?"

Titus reaches for the lone item on the compact kitchen table. "You subscribe to *Indian Country*?" Titus slides the folded newspaper in front of Charlie.

"Can't say that I do," Charlie responds, his words clipped as his cell phone buzzes in his chest pocket again, causing him to flinch. "I'm sorry."

Charlie flips his hands up in embarrassment and digs for his phone. He sees the caller is Nat. "Hello," he answers.

"Hi, Uncle Charlie," Nat's tone sounds as if he is annoyed.

"I'm kinda busy," Charlie talks into the phone, making eye contact with Titus across the table.

"Oh," Nat speaks quickly. "Tell Grandpa to quit calling me. He's already called me five times. I can't answer the phone. I'm in school."

"Why are you calling me on your phone now, when you're in school?" Charlie questions.

"I'm between classes...never mind. Just tell Grandpa to chill."

"Ok," Charlie chuckles. "When he calls me, I will tell him to, as you say, 'chill.' Bye."

Charlie tucks his phone in his pocket and holds his hands up in surrender. "I apologize."

"That's ok." Titus lets loose a laugh. "You're a popular guy." He taps on the paper. "Check out page four."

Charlie unfurls the paper and thumbs to page four. "What am I looking for?"

"You'll see it."

The black and white photo at the top of the page is a landscape shot of dancers in costume at a pow wow. The caption reads: "Dancers at the Rushmore Center were in full regalia for opening ceremonies." In the far left corner of the photo, Charlie spots a dancer dressed in a pronghorn costume. He wears the head of the animal as a hat, the hide of the animal is in strips, the photo has frozen the image perfectly capturing the dancer in stride with prongs of the pronghorn jutting beautifully skyward as the eyes of the head appear to be looking into the camera. The hide billows out in waves, giving life and movement to the photo. "Wow," Charlie whispers, "that is a great photo." He turns to Titus. "You think this is our pronghorn?"

"Think?" Titus blanches, "I know it is. I made some calls." He points a finger at the paper. "That gentleman dressed as a pronghorn, thathókala, that is Billy Joe Seeking Water. You know, the Seeking Water clan that I mentioned in your visit up here with your dad."

"Oh, yeah," Charlie whispers huskily, embarrassed.

"You're welcome," Titus growls. "That's two cases I've solved for you."

"Thank you. Thank you very much," Charlie voices his sincere gratitude.

"You're welcome." Titus smiles and waves away his contrived anger. "Just a coincidence in the *Indian Country Today* newspaper. Kinda spooky when I saw it."

Chompers rolls on the floor, emitting a growling-meow that draws the attention of both men. Titus laughs. "Old Chompers enjoying the morning sunshine."

Charlie closes the newspaper and folds it. His exaggerated straightening of the paper frightens the cat on the floor, and it leaps in the air and runs to the far side of the living room, seeking cover behind the couch. Titus laughs at the cat. "He's nervous. Probably just realized how relaxed he was in the sunbeam, and you brought him back to reality."

Charlie freezes momentarily, looking toward the cat crouching behind the sofa with only its head sticking out, eyes wide, searching the room. He stands, holding the paper up with one hand. "You mind if I take this?"

Titus waves a hand, "Be my guest. Bag it for evidence as they say on TV." He laughs.

"I'll take it and give it to the game wardens." Charlie frowns. "I'm sure they are going to be having a conversation with Billy Joe Seeking Water."

"Gotta do what they gotta do." Titus nods, his sentence punctuated with the buzz of Charlie's phone.

"Gol dang it," Charlie grumbles as he digs his phone from his breast pocket. He looks at the caller identification but doesn't recognize the number. He hesitates before pressing the button to answer. "LeBeau," he speaks crisply.

"Hi, Charlie." Charlie's head cocks, not recognizing the voice. "It's Courtney German." Charlie can hear a muffled whimper from the other end.

"Are you ok? What's wrong?" Charlie's police instincts kick into high gear at the indication of the woman crying.

"Can you come to my house?" Courtney's voice pleads mournfully.

"What's wrong?' Charlie demands.

"It's Rodney," she replies.

Charlie's blood runs cold. "You stay where you are. I'll be there in forty-five minutes."

Chapter 35

Cold Sweat, Heated Exchange

Charlie tries to control his breathing as he drives his BIA police Tahoe, lights flashing, his speeds pushing eighty-five miles per hour. His leisurely drive back to Sisseton that he had planned was thwarted by the phone call from Courtney. The rest of the morning had been set; he was going to take South Dakota Highway 25 west of Veblen then south through Hillhead and then to Lake City. From there he wanted to take a drive through Eden and check on the progress of the Catholic Church rebuilding effort. Less than a year after the fire that burned the historic church to the ground, the new foundations were supposedly being poured, at least that was the rumor that Charlie had heard. He wanted to see for his own eyes the start of the reconstruction and maybe the beginning of the healing process. But, not today. His plans are derailed by Courtney's distressed voice; he could hear the tears in her speech. What had Rodney done? She wouldn't call 911 as Charlie had insisted, so what was her emergency that wasn't an emergency? Charlie's imagination runs wild.

His mind wanders to the plan to check out Eden then drive by Buffalo Lake and see if anyone was fishing, all that is out the window. Now Charlie told himself to focus on driving. He is pushing the envelope of safe speeds and can't afford to lose his concentration and let his mind wander from the task at hand. He tells himself to keep breathing, but his thoughts drift to Courtney's urgent beckoning. Something bad has happened, and she won't say it on the phone. It wasn't like her to be so emotionally vulnerable, not that he ever remembered. That was years ago, the voice in his head chides him.

Maybe something has happened to her mother. Her mom is sick, dementia. Maybe that is part of it. Charlie's phone buzzes in his pocket; he touches his chest but decides he better not answer as he speeds down the highway. It buzzes two quick vibrations indicating somebody has left a voicemail. Two more miles down the road it buzzes again, and another voicemail is left. Another call and Charlie concedes; he slows the vehicle and extracts his phone from his breast pocket. It's Skip. He ignores the call and inspects his missed calls. One call from Nat and one call from Claude. "Dang these guys. Maybe phones aren't a good idea after all," Charlie grumbles out loud. He feels a bead of sweat on his brow as he tosses his phone aside into the cup holder, and he steps down on the accelerator.

He finally reaches Sisseton, retracing his earlier route from this morning. His lights part traffic through town along South Dakota Highway 10 as he hastily makes his way past Main Street and finally past the police station where he hangs a left onto BIA Route 7. Again his foot is heavy on the accelerator as the Tahoe cruises southbound.

Charlie can feel his heart beating faster as he pushes the vehicle past Tiospa Zina School, and he has a sense that the coffee has been processed and he needs to pee. At the intersection of BIA Route 7 and BIA Route 200, Charlie decides to make a short detour down the dirt road just beyond the Big Coulee District Community Center. He finds a clump of trees and stops. He relieves himself and is back in the vehicle just a couple of miles from Courtney's house. He tries to compose himself the best he can in the few minutes drive from the Big Coulee Community Center to the cul-de-sac in front of her house.

Hustling from his vehicle to the door, Charlie wipes at the beads of sweat on his brow, his breathing controlled. He knocks on the door and turns the knob letting himself in. "Hello," he calls out as he enters.

Courtney emerges from the back hallway that leads to the bedrooms. "Are you ok?" Charlie puts his hand on his gun. "Is he still here?" His free hand points to the floor.

Courtney's head shakes and she approaches, her face twisted as she is about to cry. Charlie cradles her face in his hands inspecting her for any sign of injury. He sees none and is puzzled as the woman thrusts herself into his arms and holds him sobbing. "What happened? What is going on? Are you hurt?" Charlie questions.

Her head shakes, and Charlie pushes her away, holding onto her arms, rubbing them, trying to calm her. "Rodney? Where is he?"

"Gone," Courtney manages to sob and points to several papers on the kitchen table. "I'm sorry. Look at me I'm a mess."

"Courtney, I don't understand," Charlie speaks firmly. "You have to tell me what's going on."

Courtney leads him to the table. "It's Rodney. He's gone. He just left. He told me he wants to give Haley to me. He gave me some papers that he signed, saying she's mine if I want her."

Charlie flips through the handwritten papers, noting the signatures at the bottom. "He gave you his kid?" Charlie questions.

"It's so sad." Courtney's eyes flow with tears. "He told me he couldn't take it. Cassandra. Denise. Both dead." She shakes her head in disbelief. "He begged me to take Haley. He said he wanted to get far away before he ruined her life too."

Charlie takes Courtney's hand and pulls out a chair at the table. "Sit down. Do you have coffee?"

Courtney nods.

"Come on, I could use some coffee too. I'll get it."

Charlie finds mugs, and pours coffee from the pot, delivering them to the table where he sits down. "So, he's gone, just like that? Not even saying goodbye to her?"

"He told me he went to the school and said goodbye." Courtney wipes her eyes with a tissue and sips her coffee. "It is just so sad!" her chest heaves spastically as she tries to hold back her sob.

Charlie re-examines the papers noting the words "custody" and "parental consent" scattered throughout the hand-written notes on lined papers, likely from Haley's notebook. The bottom of the page is signed by Rodney and a witness. Charlie can't make out the name; it looks like Phil Van Meeter, but the name is not familiar to him.

"Oh, Charlie, that poor little girl. Rodney said she didn't even bat an eye. She's had it so tough. I guess she knew it was coming." Courtney is slowly regaining her composure.

Charlie sighs and looks out the window. From the position of the house located about an eighth of the way up the Coteau, he can see across the flat prairie crop land. It is a beautiful location he notes to himself. The dire emergency he imagined on his drive over has been dispelled. The urgency is not as his anxiety reflected, and Charlie breathes deeply, recovering his demeanor. His phone buzzes in his pocket snapping him back from his recovery. It is Claude again, and he ignores the call and returns his gaze to the window.

"I want her, Charlie," Courtney demands authoritatively. "I want to take care of her. That's why I'm so emotional about this. I...I don't want her to go into foster care, when I can take care of her. I can adopt her. There's no reason she can't just stay right here. Have a home right here with me." Charlie nods. "Can you help me? Can you go to social services? What can I do?"

"I'll help you," Charlie reassures. "I'll do what I can."

A shaky voice calls from the back bedroom, "Courtney."

"It's my mom." Courtney stands, prompting Charlie to stand. "No, no. Sit. I'll be right back." Before Charlie can sit, Courtney wraps her arms around him, surprising him with a hug.

He pats her on the back. "It's ok," he whispers.

"Courtney," the voice calls again from the back room.

Courtney turns her face up to Charlie and starts to kiss him, but Charlie backs away. "Whoa." Charlie breaks the hug.

"Oh my God," Courtney yells, "I'm so sorry. I'm just so emotional. I'm sorry. I'm sorry." She darts down the hallway to attend to her mother, face in her hands, embarrassed.

Charlie sits back down and sips his coffee. His mind dismisses Courtney's reaction as he contemplates getting Haley settled. After a few minutes, Courtney slinks back to the table and sits covering her face. "I'm so embarrassed. You have to understand..."

"Don't worry about it." Charlie smiles and waves his hand. "Haley's in school then?"

"Yes," Courtney nods.

"So, nobody really knows anything about Rodney leaving?"

"Not that I know of." Courtney shakes her head.

"Well." Charlie takes a deep breath. "That's probably good. We'll have some time. Nobody is even paying attention to Rodney and his whereabouts. Not that anybody ever did to begin with." Charlie half-heartedly smiles at Courtney who returns her own pained grin. "We can quietly set you up as a foster home provider. Get you on the list. I can talk to social services and see what needs to be done."

"You can do that?" Courtney questions.

"I think so. We can probably see a judge in a closed session and complete any paperwork within a couple months to make it official. But, we won't advertise anything that's going on now." Charlie cocks his head. "What about Haley's mother?"

"Rodney said she was dead." Courtney shrugs.

"We'll have to verify that. That's the one thing that could blow this all up," Charlie says quietly. "Sooner the better. It'd be nice to get you recognized with official guardianship for school and any other requirement."

"I don't know how to thank you Charlie." Courtney's eyes well with tears. "You don't know what this means to me." Charlie can't help but notice how beautiful she still looks even in distress. Her white peasant blouse and blue jeans fit her perfectly. He digs for his phone. "You know what, I'm gonna get photos of all these papers from Rodney. I'll show them to Kendra at Social Services. She'll probably end up with the case anyway, but maybe she can give me some advice off the record." Courtney nods as Charlie snaps a photo of each paper. "Hold onto these papers, keep 'em safe."

"Do you think it will be ok?" Courtney questions.

"Yes." Charlie chuckles a bit. "Things like this...they work out." Charlie reaches across the table and pats her hand. "Did Rodney say where he's going?"

"He wasn't sure." Courtney shakes her head. "He said something about Texas."

Charlie frowns. "I don't think it even matters. I am assuming he'll wind up dead or back in prison." Charlie sighs. "With all that's happened...I guess...this is probably all for the best." Charlie breathes a half-hearted laugh. "I'll give him credit for recognizing his weakness and trying to at least think of his daughter."

Charlie stands, "You think I could use your restroom; coffee seems to have gone right through me."

"Sure." Courtney stands. "I'll show you, and I'll check on my mom again." She leads Charlie to the bathroom and heads to her mother's bedroom.

*   *   *

Charlie relieves himself and as he washes his hands he can hear a heated exchange through the thin walls of the government built, low-bid home. It's Courtney and her mother arguing in raised voices. Charlie cracks the door and listens, not knowing if he should intrude. "Did you tell him?" Courtney's mother's voice is agitated and loud.
"You have to tell him! He needs to know!"

"Mom." Courtney tries to calm her mother. She speaks with a soothing tone, "Now's not the time."

"That man out there is your daughter's father. He has a right to know. He needs to know."

Charlie's heart skips a beat. He opens the door and eases down the hall. He looks into the room where an elderly, bedridden woman wags a finger at Courtney. "If you don't tell him, I will. Sir!" The lady calls out.

"Shhh," Courtney urges. Her eye catches Charlie in the hallway looking in the room. She bolts from the room, pulling the door shut behind her.

"Courtney," her mother yells, her voice muffled behind the closed door.

"Charlie, I'm sorry. My mother has dementia. She doesn't know what she's saying."

Charlie's head spins. He turns, staggering a bit towards the living room, Courtney holding his arm. "Are you ok?"

In the living room, behind Charlie's puzzled face, his mouth struggles to form a question. "Was she referring to me? Was she saying I am your daughter's father?"

"Charlie..." Courtney grabs hold of Charlie's arms. "She doesn't know what she's saying."

Charlie's head shakes. "You're lying to me. You tell me the truth right now! I have a right to know."

"Charlie, it's so complicated."

"Just tell me," Charlie demands.

Courtney's head drops. She stares at the floor. "We didn't know until Brittney was four. She had appendicitis. There was confusion with her blood type. It led to the divorce.   Larry didn't know. I didn't know." Courtney's head shakes as she looks to her feet. Her body trembles. "I met Larry on the rebound, immediately after we split up." Courtney refuses to make eye contact. "When I went to the Cities, I got pregnant...well you know. But, I was already pregnant." Courtney begins to cry again. "I'm so sorry, Charlie. I should have told you." Courtney finally locks eyes with Charlie.

Charlie stumbles to the couch, he sits, sickened. "I can't believe this." Charlie holds his chest. "I think I might be sick." He breathes shallow breaths.

Courtney puts her hand on his back, "Take deep breaths." She pats his back. "You got to believe me; this is all some crazy mistake. I never meant for this to be anything, a burden to you...anyone."

"No, it's ok." Charlie tries to maintain his breathing. "It's just so overwhelming. It's just…" Charlie breathes. Courtney kneels down in front of him a moment, but stands quickly, "Let me get you some water."

She moves to the kitchen, and Charlie stares at the floor, flustered and confused. Courtney returns with a glass of water, and Charlie gulps it down. Courtney wipes at her eyes. "I'm so sorry to spring this on you today of all days."

She moves to the back room and disappears for a moment. She emerges carrying a folder. "I was going to tell you. I swear," Courtney whispers softly. She hands a folder to Charlie. He opens the stiff folder and finds a medical printout indicating blood type. Beneath the paper are a dozen photos. They include Brittney's school pictures and several other photos including one of her playing basketball. Charlie spends an extra moment examining the basketball photo.

"It was obvious when she had a basketball in her hand," Courtney sniffles. "She is like her father when it comes to sports." Courtney's hands shake as she kneels again and grabs Charlie's forearms. "Oh, my God. I am so sorry. I know this is a lot to take in."

Charlie's phone buzzes in his shirt pocket, and he closes the folder full of photos and digs out his phone. It is Skip. "Hello," he answers it. "Yeah, I'll be there no later than one o'clock." Charlie stands and hands the folder back toward Courtney. "I gotta go. That was the captain….Captain Kipp…you know Skip."

Courtney holds up her hand. "You can keep those photos if you like. I was setting them aside for when I told you…I guess now you know." She heaves a sigh and tears roll down her cheeks. "I am so sorry, Charlie. This isn't what I…"

Charlie nods. He stretches his arms out and hugs the shrinking woman in front of him. "I…I…I really don't know what to say." Charlie moves to the front door. "We'll talk, but I have to go now."

A Charlie LeBeau Mystery

Chapter 36

Pierre

Pierre, South Dakota, is the king of mispronunciation. Instead of conforming to a traditional interpretation one would use for a young Frenchman, Pierre, a two syllable word (pee-air) somehow the capitol city of South Dakota became identified by a single syllable word pronounced like a large boat dock, pier. It's hard to explain, but that's the way it is, in colloquialisms. Pierre, South Dakota, has roots with the French in that French explorers and trappers showed up in the early 1700's. Most notably and historically significant is the Verendrye Monument that marks the lead plate buried by the Verendrye brothers, Chevalier and Louis, claiming the land for France in 1743. The plate was located on the west side of the Missouri River that is now Fort Pierre, South Dakota. It wasn't discovered until 1913 by kids playing on the windy hillside. The discovery rewrote much of the idea of the time frames of early contact with Native Americans in the heart of the unexplored Indian country of the United States.

Pierre, South Dakota, still has deep roots connecting the Native American culture to modern times. The Crow Creek and Lower Brule Indian Reservations are located just a few dozen miles from South Dakota's capitol city, and the Native census data reflects the Lakota population in its numbers. Pierre and Fort Pierre are typical old west river cities with bluffs on each side of the river and development basically concentrated in the floodplain of the muddy Mo, the Missouri River. Flooding has not been a serious threat since the 1960's, ever since one of the largest earthen dams, the largest at the time it was built, was constructed on the Missouri River just north of town. The Oahe Dam formed the Oahe Reservoir behind it, and was dedicated by John F. Kennedy on August 17, 1962. The geography that now includes the reservoir, gives the Pierre area a solid claim to a world class sportsman's paradise. Fishing, big game hunting, and waterfowl hunting play significant roles in the economics of the area. It is a beautiful area, a reflection of the diversity of South Dakota. Winters can be severe with cold and snow, matching the intensity of the heat of summer and wicked thunderstorms. South Dakota's capitol competes for the most sparsely populated capitol in the country coming in second to Montpelier, Vermont, which can only muster about 8,000 residents, while Pierre, combined with Fort Pierre, tallies around 13,000 people.

Geographically centered in the state, Pierre is a hub of many highways: US 83, US 14, South Dakota Highway 1806 on the west side of the Missouri River and South Dakota Highway 1804 on the east side of the Missouri. These high-numbered highways commemorate the years of Lewis and Clark's epic exploration of the Louisiana Purchase. South Dakota Highway 34 also passes through the community. Fort Pierre and Pierre are connected by a 1,500 foot long steel girder bridge with a concrete deck that spans the Missouri River. In downtown Pierre you find probably the second most dominant building in Pierre, the Federal Building, second only to the state capitol building, which sits less than a mile away. At a junction of South Pierre Street, US 14, US 83, and South Dakota Highway 34, the federal building sits next to an economic landmark of the community, Lynn's Dakotamart. Dakotamart is the one stop shop for everything grocery and hunting or fishing related. Business booms year round, but especially now. The walleyes are biting; the first fall upland bird seasons are underway. Pickups with boats on trailers crowd the terraced parking lot night and day.

The federal building next to Dakotamart houses the Federal Bureau of Investigation offices and is the home office for Agent Austin Brown. Agent Brown works at his computer in his cubical on the top floor of the four story building. He is winding down his Friday afternoon with a summary of his activities for the week typed into Standard Form SF-W110, a Microsoft Word template that Brown has come to loathe. It makes him think of the conversation he has been promising to have with Jeanie, his wife. As he had discussed with Charlie before he left Sisseton, work in South Dakota, particularly on the Indian reservations has been wearing him thin. Maybe it is time to leave. Get back to civilization and out of the sparsely populated Dakotas. Nothing would be quick at this point, the kids had just started the school year and were less than two months into their elementary school semester. No, any move would be in the summer, between grades for the kids schooling. No sense in making a move more traumatic for the children by making them start at a new school mid-year. That would be cruel.

Jeanie Brown, wife of FBI Agent Austin Brown, is right next door to her husband this afternoon, doing the grocery shopping at Dakotamart. The four paper sacks full of groceries are delivered via a custom conveyor system. Jeanie drives her minivan through the parking lot to the conveyor and, handing over her plastic, numbered placards, the bagboy plucks the paper bags from the appropriately numbered tubs and places them in the back of the van. The forty year old Jeanie Brown is attractively average. Her long sandy-brown hair is pulled into a ponytail. She is slim and pretty with no makeup required. She sports large, circular, knock-off designer sunglasses that she has to lift to look at and see the screen of her cell phone. With the rear door of the van firmly slammed closed, she pulls away from the grocery conveyor, heading for the parking lot exit. Her mind is filled with the remainder of the day's chores, including picking up the kids from school next.

Almost four hundred yards away, a stranger sits in a beat-up, 1970's Ford, three-quarter ton pickup. The middle-aged, curly-haired man with a full, bushy, unruly-looking beard streaked with gray watches Jeanie through binoculars. He stows the cheap binoculars under the driver's seat and dons a motorcycle helmet with a full face shield. He buckles the chin strap of the helmet and fastens his seat belt. He starts the truck and the big 450 cubic inch, V-8 engine rumbles at an idle. He places the truck in gear and holds the brake in place ready to move. He waits, parked on Pleasant Drive, just north and west of Lynn's. Through his previous scouting over the last two weeks, he knows Jeanie will be momentarily heading through the intersection just a quarter mile in front of him.

Jeanie eases her Honda Odyssey minivan out of the parking lot and onto South Central Avenue heading north. She hums along to the country song on the radio. It's Joe Diffie singing about "A Night to Remember."

The man watches from his Ford truck and lifts his foot from the brake, stomping on the accelerator, and racing the faded, metallic green truck towards the intersection. Jeanie is moving slowly as she tries to work her cell phone, attempting to dial her husband. She takes her time bouncing over the railroad tracks at a snail's pace immediately between the parking lot turnout and the intersection of Pleasant Drive and South Central Avenue. The rough rail crossing bounces her fingers off the send button for a moment as she stops at the four-way intersection. She presses the call button and puts the phone to her ear. "Hi, Honey. I'm just leaving Lynn's," she speaks cheerfully into the phone as Austin Brown answers. "Will you be home for supper by six? I got some pork chops."

After pausing at the four way stop sign, Jeanie enters the intersection and is hit broadside in the driver's door by the pickup truck traveling at just under fifty-five miles per hour.

Chapter 37

Broadside

Sitting in his office cubical, Agent Austin Brown's senses are dulled from the long day at the office, scuffling with paperwork. He relaxed even a little when he saw his wife's number on the caller ID and a touch more when he heard the love-of-his-life's voice. He doesn't even have time to respond to a simple question about supper. The ear-splitting crunch of metal-on-metal causes him to pull the phone from his ear, juggle it, and almost drop his cell phone to the floor.

Agent Brown's chair skitters away on its rollers as he bolts upright. "Honey? Honey!" he yells into his phone, scrambling out of his cubicle, knocking over a stack of folders precariously balanced on the corner of his desk. He appears to be playing out the dance of a lunatic, moving from the open area of his office, past the elevator bay and to the empty offices of the northeast corner of the building. He can see the Dakotamart parking lot below, and the intersection of South Central Avenue and Pleasant Drive a short distance from the store. A couple hundred yards away, two steaming vehicles and a debris field litter the street. An old truck appears to have nearly split his family minivan in half.

Brown's hands shake as he attempts to dial 911; his fingers failing to cooperate efficiently, he needs several tries to hit the correct buttons. There is no movement amongst the wreckage in the distance. He bolts from the window just before a man crawls from the window of the pickup truck.

*　　*　　*

On the street, out of the wreckage a man gingerly wriggles out the crushed window of the Ford truck, staggering a couple steps away from the mangled vehicles, stretching casually, and feeling the impact of the crash, he rubs the bruise across his chest where the shoulder seatbelt dug in. He removes his helmet and tosses it into the bed of the truck. He moseys away down the sidewalk, heading north on Central Avenue before turning east on Capitol Avenue, seemingly without a care in the world.

*   *   *

It's a blur for Agent Austin Brown. He makes decisions quickly. Bypassing the elevators he sprints down the stairs. He relays the information to the 911 dispatcher the best he can under breathless conditions. His focus is broken by the sound of a siren as he dashes across the Dakotamart parking lot, up the embankment of the railroad tracks, and finally to South Central Avenue. He can see the Pierre City Police car and its strobing lights flashing in the intersection. The van has been hit with such force that it rests upside-down on its roof. The truck then came to rest against the undamaged side of the van. A police officer is at the window of the van attempting to tend to the woman buckled in her seat belt, hanging upside down. She is unconscious. The stomping steps of a gasping of Agent Brown draw the officer's attention as more sirens squeal in the distance. The policeman attempts to hold back Brown. "Sir!" he yells. He shouts orders at the running man, "Stay back!"

Brown has his FBI credentials out of his jacket pocket on the run. He moves his mouth, but nothing except for gasps come out. The police officer grabs hold of the FBI agent, preventing him from getting closer. Brown rips away from his grip. "Sir, stay away from her!"

"This is my wife!" Agent Brown shouts at the man, before turning his attention to his unconscious wife hanging, suspended upside down by her seatbelt, arms hanging limply from her shoulder. He kneels and touches her face. The side of her head is red and swollen, a trickle of blood runs into her hair, forming a small red circle on in her hairline.

The policeman is at Brown's side again; he kneels, "I am sorry, sir. Please just wait for the paramedics. She's alive. I checked, but we shouldn't touch her."

"This is my wife! I'm with the FBI!" Brown flashes his badge again. Adrenaline courses through his body. "I will wait until the paramedics arrive." He pushes down the deflated side-curtain air bag and gently touches her cheek. "It's ok, Honey," he whispers. "I'm here. You're gonna be ok."

A minute passes and the fire department along with an ambulance arrives with medical technicians. The police officer grabs Brown by the arm. "Sir, please, let's move and let them do their jobs."

The paramedic quickly fastens a collar to Jeanie, immobilizing her neck. The door is crushed to a point that the firemen have to use the Jaws-of-Life to rip it off its hinges. In a matter of minutes she is cut from the seatbelt and gently moved to a stretcher. She groans as a hint of consciousness flashes. Her left leg is immobilized along with her left arm, both appear to be broken. She is loaded into the ambulance, and Agent Brown follows her into the vehicle. He hunches over and kneels next to her, holding her good hand. Jeanie groans and Austin Brown squeezes his wife's hand. Her eyes flutter open. "Shhh," Agent Brown urges. "Don't try to talk, Honey. You're safe."

Her eyes twitch back and forth, and she groans again, squeezing Agent Brown's hand tightly. "It's ok," Brown whispers. "You're on the way to the hospital."

Chapter 38

Blindside

Agent Brown feels some relief with his wife in the hospital under the care of an emergency room doctor. He paces in the waiting room. He has already made the call to Becky, Jeanie's best friend, and she has picked up the kids from school and is watching them. It's forty-five minutes before the doctor emerges from the ER and briefs Agent Brown. The FBI agent notes the doctor seems young, probably barely thirty years old. He is dressed in the blue scrubs, including a matching blue skull cap. His eyes look tired behind the 1980's style, brown, plastic-framed glasses. "Mr. Brown?" he questions in the waiting area. There are only three other people in the compact space, furnished with uncomfortable, straight-backed chairs and their worn, padded cushions.

"Mm-hmm," Brown answers sidling over to the doctor, who swipes the skull cap from his head, revealing fine, thinning, brown hair.

The doctor heaves a sigh. "She's out of danger for the moment. Broken arm. Broken leg. We believe she has some internal bleeding. Spleen probably." He points to the desk at the nurses' station across the waiting room. "You're going to have sign the release for surgery. We're going to go in to stop the bleeding."

Brown stares at the doctor's mouth, watching the words emerge from the back of his throat. Brown nods his head ever so slightly.

"Right away," the doctor whispers."

The doctor puts his hand on the agent's shoulder. "She's very lucky. The *next generation* side-curtain air bags saved her." He drops his arm and turns back to the ER. "We're taking her to surgery right now."

"Thank you, Doctor." Brown nods.

The doctor frowns, "It's gonna be a few hours before she's awake. You got family, kids?"

Brown nods.

"Why don't you go home, be with your kids. You'll see her when she's out of recovery."

Agent Brown nods; his face is expressionless. His mind turns over everything that's happened. He watches the back of the doctor disappear into the ER. The hospital is a little over a mile from his office, and he walks out the door heading northwest along Sioux Avenue, the main drag through Pierre. He wants answers. He walks with a purpose. What about the other driver? Brown is oblivious to the heavy afternoon traffic as school is out, and others are getting off work. In a few minutes he is past his office, striding to the crash site. The family van is upright and on the back of a flatbed truck. He asks the driver, "Where are you taking the vehicle?"

The truck driver hands him a card. "All the info's on there," the middle-aged man replies.

Brown nods and turns his attention to the smashed pickup truck. A different flatbed truck works to hook chains to the mangled heap of metal. He approaches a policeman, extracts his FBI credentials, and shows them to the officer near the pickup truck. "What can you tell me about the truck and driver?"

The officer looks around nervously having never seen an FBI agent before. He stammers, "Uh-uh, um, nothing, Sir. The truck was reported stolen a week ago." The officer looks at his notepad. "It's registered to a David Bad Moccasin. He has a ranch down on Lower Brule." The officer shakes his head in disgust. He frowns. "Seen this before. Probably some drunk Indian. Just walked off to who knows where. Unhurt, probably."

FBI Agent Austin Brown stares at the officer. "So, no driver?"

"Nope." The officer shakes his head. "Nobody saw nothing."

Brown's attention is focused on the store behind the officer. He begins to walk towards the building, drawn like a moth to a flame. It's an investment brokerage office, American Mutual the sign indicates. It's a nice, well kept, brick building, but most importantly there is a video camera at the entrance. Brown is mesmerized as he approaches the entrance of the building. He turns and holds his hands out gauging the field of view the camera might have. Yes, the camera probably picked up the crash. He yanks open the door of the office as a secretary at the front desk calls out, "We're closing, Sir." She's young, attractive, and dressed professionally.

Agent Brown pulls his FBI credentials again from his pocket. "Did you see the crash out here?" he questions, pointing his free hand to the street.

The young lady stammers, "I-I-I…" She can't speak, intimidated by the badge.

Brown tucks his badge back in his pocket. "Never mind about the crash. Is that camera working out there?" He points to the entrance. "The one at your entrance?"

"Yes," the lady nods.

"Does it record?"

"Yes," she nods her head. "It goes on the computer. We had some vandalism, some graffiti, so we put up security measures."

"Can I see it? This was a hit and run crash out here, and we're looking for the driver."

"Sure." The young lady waves Brown around the low partition and points him to a monitor and keyboard. "Just hit the mouse, and the screen should come up."

Brown sits at the computer and moves the mouse. Sure enough, an image comes up with multiple views of the outside of the building. "Just click on the view you want. A controller will appear, and you can rewind and freeze-frame. We've had to do this for police because of the vandalism before."

Brown clicks on the front entrance view. It is a black and white recording of images taken every two seconds or so. The jerky playback proceeds in reverse very quickly, and it is obvious when the crash happens and he stops the image. Pressing the arrow on the screen with his mouse, he lets the video go forward. The stop-action photo animation reminds Brown of the TV show *South Park*, with its crude movements.

It's a wave of nausea that follows. Coming over the agent like a bucket of ice water poured atop his head, the dizziness, cold sweat, and shallow breaths hit him. He is hyperaware of his body, and he pauses the video. He glances at the lady looking over his shoulder a moment before swallowing hard and looking at the screen. He wonders if the woman notices his distress. He concentrates on not falling out of his chair. He widens his feet on the floor and grabs the desk with both hands in front of him. "Are you alright?" the woman whispers behind him.

Agent's Brown question is answered; yes, she did notice his distress. He lies, "I'm fine." He reaches for his phone. "I just want to get a photo of this person on the screen. I think it's our driver of the hit and run." He points a finger at the girl. "Whatever you do, don't delete this video.

We're going to need this as evidence." The woman nods obediently. Brown snaps the photo on his phone. He immediately views it in his gallery of photos. He pinches his fingers on the screen and then stretches them, enlarging the photo. There is no denying it. It is the Deer Slayer. This is the serial killer that he hunted, along with Charlie, two years ago. The cold-blooded killer had gotten away. Brown shakes his head in disbelief. It was him, Elliot Koffman. His hair was long and curly, and his beard looked like something a mountain man would sport.

Agent Brown pockets his phone and returns to the video. He rewinds the video to the crash and lets it play out. It is a little far away, but it is clear. The man getting out the truck is Elliot. He was wearing a helmet, but he removed it and tossed it in the back of the truck before nonchalantly walking away.

Brown bolts upright in his chair, he digs in his pocket and pulls out several business cards. He peels one from the group and shakily hands it to the lady. "Remember, don't lose that video. I have to go." The woman nods, and Brown is out the door.

He runs to the flatbed loading the pickup. "Wait! Wait!" he yells waving his arms. The man working the winch, dragging the vehicle up the tilted bed, stops as he sees the FBI agent running at him. Brown has his badge out and is leaping into the back of the truck before the man can say anything.

"You supposed to be up there?" the man at the winch questions.

"Just collecting some evidence," Brown replies reassuringly. "FBI evidence."

The helmet is in plain sight on top of a coil of barbed wire and a few metal fence posts. The black, shiny helmet is a perfect blotter for fingerprints. In a few minutes Brown knows he will have confirmation that this hit-and-run driver is Elliot. He knows that means it likely wasn't an accident. No, his wife had been a target. But, why? Brown's anger starts to boil. Why would this cold-blooded killer make such a brazen attack in broad daylight? Any answer he imagines brings chills to his bones, while simultaneously bringing his blood to a boil.

Chapter 39

Sinking

Big Coulee Community – Near Sisseton, South Dakota

He is sick to his stomach as he drives. Charlie is a distracted driver as he heads north, departing from Courtney's house and the Big Coulee District headed back to Sisseton. It is overwhelming...he has child? How could an average, everyday change his life in an instant so drastically? The words bounce around his head. Courtney was practically hysterical, but she was clear that Brittney had not been told who her real father is. She promised that she would wait for Charlie to absorb the news before discussing it further...with anyone. It's a miracle that Charlie stays on the road. He is not even conscious of his driving. Past the community college, past Tiospa Zina High School, he drives under the speed limit, oblivious to anything other than his thoughts and trying to recall the ten years previous, the time Courtney and he split. There had been a couple of overnight trips to visit her in Minneapolis, at her house that she shared with three other girls just on the edge of the University of Minnesota campus. As Charlie recalls with a smile, most of the time had been spent in bed locked in her bedroom, disturbed once in a while by one of the roommates wanting to know if they wanted to go get something to eat. The answer was always no.

The long distance romance didn't work out, as these things tend not to. Immediate and constant attention is often needed at such a critical time in a relationship, and the five hour drives took their toll. They split amicably, almost without a word about a break up. It was just moving on. Phone calls trickled down from once a day, to a couple times a week, then none. Plans weren't made. It was over. One final fling on his last Minneapolis visit left them both with smiles on their faces. Yes, it was completely mutual. That's when it must have happened. Impregnated in their farewell goodbye, it was beyond Charlie's imagination.

Through the gossip in Sisseton, Charlie knew she had found a new boyfriend right away. The rumor was that she had the new beau months before Charlie and Courtney called it quits. He never had any reason to suspect that he had fathered her child. She was on birth control pills. At least that's what she told him. How could this have happened? But more so, how could she not have known she might have been pregnant when they split? It bothered him that she seemingly never knew that the man she had married wasn't even her baby's daddy...not until an emergency appendectomy. How does such a secret occur in today's society? Charlie shakes his head in bewilderment, suddenly aware that he's on the outskirts of Sisseton.

What was he going to do? Should he tell Veronica right away? No. He can't do that. He has to think about how to break the news and be gentle about it. "She's an awesome woman," he whispers the words out loud. "She'll understand."

Charlie heads straight for his house, not even stopping at the police station. He's not feeling well. He parks in the driveway and heads into the house.

"Hey, look who's home?" Claude greets Charlie from his recliner. The TV is muted as Claude reads the paper, he peers over his reading glasses at his son.

"Hey, Dad," Charlie mumbles.

"What's wrong? You don't look good. You look a little peaked," Claude observes with concern.

Charlie rubs his bandaged arm. The stitches itch. "I don't know what it is. I don't feel good. I'm gonna go lay down."

"Ok," Claude replies softly. "Maybe go to the casino for supper. I think it's rib night."

"I'll let you know." Charlie grimaces as he moves to his bedroom on the opposite end of the house. Charlie drops his utility belt and removes his uniform, draping everything on a chair; he crawls into bed. His mind still spins with the thoughts of Courtney and Brittney, *his daughter*. But even with his thoughts swirling his head, he's exhausted. He falls asleep.

*   *   *

Three hours later, Charlie awakens to a rapping at his door. The bedroom door opens and it's Nat. "Hey, Charlie, can you move your Tahoe? I wanna shoot some baskets."

Charlie groans pushing himself up on an elbow. "Keys are in my pocket." He points to the chair where his pants hang.

"You sure?" Nat questions. "You always say that neither Claude nor I can drive your police vehicle, no matter what."

Charlie clucks his tongue. "Just grab the keys and move it."

Nat scampers into the room, grabs the keys, and exits quickly.

Charlie falls onto his back. He stares at the ceiling and rubs his eyes with the meaty part of his hands where the thumbs connect. He's still miserable. The thoughts of having not known about his daughter nag at him. He's reminded of the saying: *One of the most difficult realizations a man has is: knowing that you don't know.* Was it Confusions that said that? His mind ponders the question. *Wisdom is knowing that you don't know.* Yes, that was the saying, and he was living it to the extreme at this moment.

He gets up and puts on shorts and his basketball shoes. Maybe a quick game of hoops with Nat would help distract him. Opening the door of his bedroom, he is greeted by the TV blasting ESPN's Sports Center. "Geez, Dad!" Charlie yells as he gets a glass and fills it with water. "Is it loud enough for you?" Sarcasm drips off the question.

"Hey, who got up on the wrong side of the bed?" Claude replies as he works the TV volume.

"I'm going to shoot with Nat." Charlie drains his glass of water. "We'll head to the casino for supper about seven. I'll see if Veronica wants to go."

Charlie and Nat play a game of horse. One player shoots, and if the basket is made, the other player shoots from that same spot. If the second shooter makes it, he's safe, but a miss will give him a letter in the word horse. First one to have all the letters that spell out horse is the loser. It's all business. Charlie wins the game, and the one-on-one game to seven begins. Charlie is not messing around. His usual happy-go-lucky trash talk is absent. He's just trying to win and he does. It's a nine to seven victory, having to win by two. The two cool down, shooting free throws in silence. It's Nat that finally has to ask, "Everything all right? You're pretty quiet."

"Yeah," Charlie responds, as he flicks his wrist on his follow through, swishing the shot. "Just a long day."

Nat tosses the ball to Charlie on the free throw line. "That's enough for me," Charlie bounces the ball back to Nat. "I'm gonna shower. We're going to the casino for supper."

"Ok." Nat dribbles the ball to the free throw line as he watches Charlie disappear into the house.

Nat shoots a few free throws and heads inside. He flops onto the couch. "Grandpa, what's up with Charlie?"

Claude's eyebrows arch, and he shrugs his shoulders. "Beats me."

* * *

Veronica joins the men for supper at the Dakota Connection, and the ribs are good. It's not a good evening for Charlie. All the food is tasteless. He is just going through the motions of eating. His thoughts are a million miles away, turning his secret over and over in the folds of his mind. "What is wrong with you?" Veronica finally asks for the third time after she notices Charlie just staring at the wall, over her head.

"Nothing," Charlie insists. He rubs his arm, squeezing the bandage. "I'm exhausted. I hope this thing's not infected."

Him, a father, Charlie still struggles with the words bouncing in his head. He is in a daze. It nags at him. He wants to blurt it out. Share his pain and confusion with Veronica. Get her opinion, help, and assistance on what to do. It's painstaking to sit casually at the table, pretending everything is fine. Tonight, Charlie thinks to himself. I'll talk to her in bed tonight. She'll stay over, so she can get up early and hunt with us. That's a good plan.

"Should we get a drink?" Veronica questions. "You look like you could use something to relax. Why are you so tense?"

"No." Charlie frowns. "I just don't feel right. I think it's my arm." Charlie massages the bandage again.

"Oh, bah." Veronica frowns and waves a dismissive hand at Charlie. "Let's get a bottle of their sweet wine. It's good for dessert. Me, you, and your dad can enjoy it."

"Fine," Charlie concedes.

Veronica orders the bottle, and a few minutes later the wine is on the table. After a quick toast to the weekend turkey hunt, the glasses are tipped back.

Veronica is good at finally drawing out Charlie from his thoughts, and he participates in the conversation that centers on the turkey hunt slated for tomorrow morning. "Danny can't make it," Nat announces. "He had told me that he would walk the coulee and see if he could push some birds to me, but he has to help his mom. They're going to paint his grandma's house this weekend. She's lives in Flandreau."

"Should be nice weather for painting," Claude acknowledges. "I'm sure Charlie and I can handle the walking. We'll scare 'em to you."

"I'm not sure you should be walking so much," Charlie cautions.

"Heck, I can walk," Veronica interjects.

"Yeah, that might be a better plan." Charlie sips his water. The meal has wound down, and they wait for the check and the to-go boxes for the leftovers. "Claude can drop us off in the morning. One of us can walk from the downstream side, and the other can walk from the upstream. The turkeys will be coming out of their roosts, and if you just walk slow, they'll mosey up ahead."

"Still don't think you can shoot yet?" Nat questions.

"Better not," Charlie shakes his head. "I definitely don't want to rip the stitches."

"That's ok with me." Nat grins. "I'll put a decoy out and when those Toms start moving, I'll give a little purr. Those suckers will come right in. Boom! Just like last week."

Charlie smiles and gives a nod to Nat. The check arrives, and Claude scoops it up. "I got this one," Claude calls out.

"You might as well stay with me tonight." Charlie puts his arm around Veronica's shoulder as they stand. "We have to be up early for the hunt."

Veronica smiles. "I suppose." She holds up her glass. "A toast to a turkey on the table tomorrow!"

"Hear, hear," Claude intones.

Charlie, Claude, and Veronica clink their glasses together along with Nat and his glass of water.

*   *   *

Charlie's clock-radio alarm sounds in the dark. The music plays Jerrod Niemann's "Lover, Lover." He clicks the switch off with a wry smile. "Oh, is it time to get up already?" Veronica groans and stretches.

Charlie snuggles close to her. "I set it an hour early. I thought we could, you know...get the day off on the right foot." The room is pitch black, and Charlie nuzzles Veronica's ear and she giggles.

"I should have known that's why you were so set on me going hunting." She kisses his mouth, and the couple shed their pajamas.

They share their bodies in a passionate session in the darkness and fall back asleep in each others arms when finished. Sleep is interrupted again by a second alarm.

"Oh boy," Veronica mumbles and shivers. "Is that the real alarm this time?" She kisses Charlie as he paws at his clock.

"What? What the heck?" Charlie questions as he looks at the clock. "It's my phone." He jumps from the bed and locates the glowing phone in his shirt pocket hanging on a chair. Veronica can see her lover's naked body in the darkness, illuminated eerily by the glow of the phone. She watches her man's tight body straighten as he sees the screen. "It's Agent Brown."

"Answer it," Veronica insists.

It is too late. "I missed it," Charlie murmurs.

"Come back to bed," Veronica whispers. "He'll call back if it's important."

The clock radio fires up its alarm. This time the radio plays Jimmy Wayne's song "Do You Believe Me Now" and Charlie turns it off. "He's calling at 5:30 in the morning; it must be important," Charlie mumbles as he climbs under the covers and cozies next to Veronica, phone still in his hand. Charlie's mind drifts again to the information Courtney shared about her daughter...his daughter. It's a sinking feeling that he can't shake. It's an emotion Charlie has never dealt with. His mind locks onto this dilemma of breaking the news to Veronica. He decides this is the time, "You ever think about kids?" Charlie asks quietly.

He can feel Veronica's body tighten as she hears the question. "Of course I have," she replies. Her hands rub Charlie's back as the lay side-by-side. Their eyes have adjusted to the darkness, and the light from the clock provides enough illumination to enable each of them to see each other's eyes, but not much else.

"I'm getting kinda old, but I'm willing to try if you are." Veronica giggles. "Emphasis on the try part."

"I'm serious," Charlie's voice is a whisper.

"I am too," Veronica insists.

"It's just that..." Charlie begins, but the conversation is shattered by the phone lighting, vibrating, and a ringtone rudely interrupting. He looks at the phone. "It's Agent Brown." Charlie presses the button answering the call. "Hello."

Chapter 40

A Cause

Charlie doesn't know what to expect. A phone call from FBI Agent Brown at 5:30 in the morning, what could it be? Too many questions clutter his thoughts. In his mind it has to be serious. "Hello?" he questions.

"Charlie." He hears on the other end.

Charlie smiles. "Agent Brown, to what do I owe the pleasure at this time of night, and on a weekend too?" The line seems dead, and Charlie questions again, "Hello?"

"Charlie," Agent Brown finally responds. "I am going to text you a photo. Look at it and call me right back."

"Ok?" Charlie's voice rises questioningly.

"Call me right back," Brown speaks quickly and the call ends.

Charlie leans over and clicks on the night table lamp. Veronica squints in pain as the light shines. "What does he want? What's happening?"

"I don't know." Charlie shrugs, confused as he stares at his phone. It buzzes and chimes indicating a text message. "Here it is. He texted me a photo. I'm supposed to look at it and call him right back."

Veronica scoffs, "Mysterious."

Charlie opens the text message and touches the attached file. A photo fills his screen. It is black and white, a little grainy but the identity of the person centered in the photo is obvious. "Holy shit," Charlie growls the words. "I don't believe this."

"What? What is it? Let me see." Veronica grabs Charlie's hand moving the phone so she can see. "Who is it?" she questions. She chokes on the words as recognition hits her. She emits a clipped scream and covers her mouth. Her eyes well with tears, and her head shakes. She pulls her hand away from her mouth. "I don't believe it. It can't be."

Charlie scrolls through his phone and pushes the button, dialing Brown. "It can't be Elliot." He looks at Veronica as he gets out of bed. He's still naked and moves to his dresser. Opening a drawer he extracts a pair of boxers and struggles to pull them up with one hand. Veronica watches Charlie hold the phone and awkwardly try to dress.

"It's him, Charlie. What are we going to do?" Veronica looks around the room nervously, as if the criminal might be lurking nearby.

"Hello," Brown answers his phone.

"He's back. The Deer Slayer. Where's the photo from?" Charlie rattles off his statements and a question.

There is silence on the phone, but Charlie can sense a sniffling. Is Brown crying? Charlie's face scrunches in question, and Veronica's follows as she questions Charlie's expression with a shrug.

"Agent Brown? Are you ok?" Charlie questions.

"It's Jeanie." Brown struggles to speak. "She was in an accident, a crash I mean."

"Oh, my God," Charlie breathes the words with a hiss. "Is she going to be ok?"

"I don't know, Charlie," Brown cries into the phone. "I'm with her in intensive care. She's in a coma. She had surgery to stop her internal bleeding." Charlie can hear the deep shaky breath of the emotional man. "She didn't wake up, Charlie."

"What happened?" Charlie questions. "I don't understand. What about the photo?"

"It was him, Charlie," Browns voice rises. "Elliot! He hit her. Hit and run. Broadside. In the middle of the day. She was on her way to get the kids from school!"

"The photo?"

Brown continues, "He was in an old junky ranch truck he stole from someone down in Lower Brule." He gulps for breath, and Charlie anxiously waits for the story to continue. "I got security video from a nearby business of the crash site. That's a photo I took from the surveillance. It was the Deer Slayer plain as day, bearded and with long hair." Brown pauses again. "He was wearing a motorcycle helmet in the truck. He took it off and tossed in the bed of the truck and walked away like he was out for a Sunday stroll. I printed the helmet. It's definitely him."

The phone goes silent. "Austin, are you ok? Kids ok?"

Brown sniffles. "I have to be ok, Charlie. Kids are with Jeanie's friend Becky. They're fine."

"What can I do? What do you need?" Charlie asks.

"Can you help me, Charlie?" Brown questions flatly.

"Sure. Anything. I'll head out right now. Do you want me to bring Veronica? She can watch the kids."

"No," Brown answers his voice gaining strength. "Jeanie's mom is flying in. I just need you. We're gonna hunt this guy down. I'm going to kill him."

"Austin," Charlie whispers his name.

"He can't do this, Charlie. I'm going to kill him."

Charlie sighs heavily. He asks a rhetorical question, "Austin, are you sure it's him?"

Brown roars into the phone, "It was him," the words are punctuated in a staccato manner. "The Deer Slayer. Elliot Koffman. I'm positive." There is a pause. "He's a dead man." Both men are silent. It drags on and Veronica slaps at Charlie, trying to understand. Brown asks, "Can you come to Pierre? I need some help. You know this guy. We know this guy. I need your help." The words trail off pleadingly.

"I'll pack up and leave right now," Charlie speaks the words reassuringly. "I'll be there in a few hours."

"Thanks, Charlie," Agent Brown's voice is full of gratitude. Charlie can hear the deep breaths again. His final words are slow and tipped with venom, "I'm goin to kill that son-of-a-bitch."

Charlie pauses. "Au-Austin," he stutters. "We'll talk about it when I get there."

Veronica is out of bed getting dressed. The volume on the phone was at a level where she got the gist of Agent Brown's side of the conversation. She looks at Charlie, and her head shakes. "I just can't believe this." She moves to Charlie and wraps her arms around him. "You should let him kill him. I sort of wish *you* would kill him. For me."

Charlie sighs and rubs Veronica's back. "I know." He takes a deep breath and breaks from her hug, "Go get those guys up and tell them what's going on. I gotta pack."

Veronica puts on her clothes and exits the bedroom, pulling the door shut behind her. Charlie's mind immediately goes back to Courtney and Brittney. He'd wait to talk to Veronica. After he gets back from Pierre, then he'd have a serious conversation with her. He shakes his head. "No," he whispers to himself. He's got to tell her now. He opens the door, and Veronica is standing on the other side, hand on the doorknob, a strange expression paints her face. "What is it?" Charlie questions.

Veronica pushes her way to into the room, closing the door behind her. "I gotta tell you something," they say in unison.

"Jinx." Veronica grins, "Go ahead, you go first."

Charlie takes a deep breath and pauses, and before he can speak, Veronica blurts out, "I'm pregnant!" Her hands go to her face and she dances/runs in place in excitement. "It's just like six weeks, but I can't believe what you said when we were in bed...about kids. What a coincidence!"

Charlie stumbles backwards to the bed. He sits on the edge of the bed, stunned into silence. Veronica approaches and climbs into his lap. "Say something." She kisses him.

Charlie's head shakes side to side as a grin creases his face. "I can't believe this. This is...great!"

Veronica hugs Charlie tightly. "What did you have to tell me?"

"Nothing," Charlie whispers. "I'll talk to you about it later. Remind me."

*　　*　　*

Small suitcase in hand, Charlie is out the door, his mind racing, thoughts bouncing from Agent Brown to Veronica. He starts his truck and heads down the driveway. "I can't do this," he mumbles aloud as he gets to the county road. He turns his truck around and heads back home.

In his driveway, the truck idles as he organizes his thoughts. The vehicle's return has drawn Veronica to the window and she parts the blinds and peers into the darkness at Charlie curiously. The truck's engine cuts off, and Charlie exits the vehicle. The slamming vehicle door brings a smile to Veronica's face. "What did he forget?" she whispers to herself.

Charlie is back inside the house marching toward Veronica. Her smile disappears as she notes his serious expression. "What is it?"

Charlie looks over his shoulder toward Claude's and Nate's bedrooms. He can see light emanating beneath the doors. Both are up getting ready to hunt.

Charlie puts a finger to his lips and points to the bedroom; he grabs Veronica's hand and leads her into his room, closing the door behind them. "I have a couple things to tell you. You better sit down."

Veronica sits on the edge of the bed, her heads spins in wonderment.

"I told you that I needed to tell you something, then I said we could talk about it later. Well, it can't wait," Charlie begins and his breath is already short. He holds out his hand. "I'm sure you noticed that I've been a little bit on edge."

Veronica laughs. "That's putting it mildly."

"I just found out, that…" Charlie can't finish his sentence.

"What is it?" Veronica stands and puts an arm around him. "Whatever it is, we can handle it. We're together. You are not facing anything alone." Worry grips her throat. "Are you sick?"

Charlie blurts out the words, "I have a daughter."

Veronica stiffens in his arms and then her knees buckle. Charlie holds her and eases her to the bed. His words are a mile a minute in clipped sentences. "I've been working with Courtney to help her with social services and Haley. All of a sudden she just bursts out crying. I thought it was because of her mom's Alzheimer's and that stress." Charlie's hands go up in the air. "Next thing I knew she was telling me about Britney's surgery when she was four years old and the discovery that her ex-husband wasn't the father."

"And she said you're the father?" Veronica questions in a monotone as the information sinks in.

"Yes," Charlie's voice is shaky. "I believe her, but I'll get tested." Charlie moves to the edge of the bed and wraps his arms around Veronica. "This doesn't change anything for you and me." He squeezes her tightly. "I just had to tell you. It was eating me alive."

Tears stream down Veronica's face. Charlie's eyes well with emotion. "We're a team. You and me," Charlie states matter-of-factly. "Starting now, you are going to live here. As soon as I get back from Pierre, you and I will get married." Charlie gets on a knee. He holds Veronica's face in his hands tenderly, looking into her eyes, "You will marry me, won't you?" he questions in a whisper.

Veronica nods and whispers, "Yes."

With a kiss the promise is sealed and Charlie heaves a sigh. "Now for the difficult stuff."

Veronica is overwhelmed with emotion, but she catches the words. "Difficult stuff? What do you mean difficult stuff?"

Charlie tries to control his breathing. He stands and paces. "Can we keep all this to ourselves for now? The baby. Brittney. Marriage."

Veronica is puzzled. "What is going on? What do you mean?"

"This Elliot business," Charlie growls the words. "You are not safe. I'm going to make sure we got eyes on you all the time until I get back."

Charlie nods. "I'm going to call Skip. We can get Jeremy. And Claude can even keep a gun close."

"Oh, my God," Veronica gasps the words. "You think he...?" The words trail off.

Charlie shakes his head. "He's already taken a run at Agent Brown's wife. I don't want to take any chances." Charlie moves to the bed again and takes a seat next to Veronica. "Let's keep all this on the down low." Veronica acknowledges the request with a nod. "Listen," Charlie tips her chin, so he can meet her eyes. "Here's an idea. Why don't we announce we're getting hitched, and we can just say we had planned everything before, but this Deer Slayer situation has expedited our plans?"

Veronica smiles. "I like that idea, Charlie."

Charlie squeezes her in his arms. "Try not to worry. You're in my protective custody, now and forever."

The couple holds their embrace for a minute, each lost in head-spinning thoughts. Charlie finally pushes back. "I gotta go. Agent Brown needs my help. It's going to be ok."

Charlie pulls away, Veronica still grasping his hand as he withdraws. His arm stretches as Veronica holds on as long as she can. "Be careful."

To be continued...

Greg Heitmann has worked for the Federal Government for 20 plus years, which pays the bills while pursuing a career in writing. His life experiences have been an inspiration for much of his writing. Look for something new from Greg soon!